The Wicked Walk

The Wicked Walk

by W . E . Mkufya

MKUKI NA NYOTA
DAR-ES-SALAAM

PUBLISHED BY
Mkuki na Nyota Publishers Ltd
Nyerere Road, Quality Plaza Building
P. O. Box 4246
Dar es Salaam, Tanzania
www.mkukinanyota.com
publish@mkukinanyota.com

© Mkuki na Nyota Publishers Ltd, 2012

First Published by Tanzania Publishing House, 1977
Mkuki na Nyota Edition, 2012

ISBN 978 9987 08 203 2

To my beloved Father

Thou shalt keep them, O Lord,
Thou shalt preserve them from this generation forever,
The wicked walk on every side, when the vilest men are exalted.

Psalms 12: 7,8

PROLOGUE

It was a beautiful, warm Dar es Salaam morning. The famous coastal music, taarab, blared from radios set at full blast. It mixed with the sounds of people yelling at each other, calling each other, exchanging nasty words and the result was one big roar. From time to time a boy would pass shouting: 'Bread for tea!' or 'Buns for breakfast!' or *'Matako ya mke!'** They were cheap and they sold nicely in this area during breakfast hours.

The whole district was a giant brothel. As Deo walked along the sandy path, he met an assortment of faces worn by shy men coming out of the whores' houses. Their clothes were shabby and shambled into uncountable folds. The greasy, unwashed faces showed white saliva solidified into broad lines extending from mouth to cheek. The hazy look on the men's faces showed self-satisfaction, but also deep exhaustion and physical weakness. There were a good number of cars parked outside the prostitutes' homes.

Deo peeped into the houses as he passed. The whores whose men had left were already preparing their breakfasts, ready to sustain the strong thrashes of the daytime customers. These houses were not very attractive. Most of them were roofed with coconut palm leaves; and those made with iron sheets were full of rust making them look like triangular anthills. The windows were purposely made small to stop some unfaithful customers from escaping in the night, paying nothing for the services. The walls of the houses were unplastered.

During the daytime trade most of the doors of the houses were wide open and each prostitute sat not very far from the door, about two or three yards from the entrance. Usually they sat on mats woven from palm leaf fibres. Their bodies facing the entrance, they observed anyone who passed nearby and welcomed everyone who peeped or knocked at the door. Those whose houses were known to many customers never sat at the door, they just waited inside and the customers would come.

---

*Meaning a woman's buttocks, which was an expression for a kind of large maize fried in oil?

Deo turned round a corner and faced the house for which he was looking. He wondered whether he would meet Nancy's mother busy with a man. He rapped lightly on the door. There was no answer. He put his ear to a crevice in the door, expecting to hear the sounds of a bed squeaking as the woman conducted her trade. No sound. He walked to a window on the side of the house and rapped with a careful gentleness. No reply. He hit it harder and harder. Still no reply, nor was there any movement that indicated the presence of people. He peeped into the room through a crack in the window. The scene inside made him gasp and dash a few yards away in fear. He kept away for some time, nursing his shock. Then softly he wiped his eyes, went forward and took a long, concerned look into the room. After observing the scene thoroughly he stepped back and cried to the neighbours for help.

When neighbours arrived they kicked open the door and rushed into the house. Inside, a naked woman dangled peacefully from a rope. She was dead.

Deo looked at Maria hanging dead, then at the assembly of neighbours, most of whom were customers of the prostitutes and he remembered the last line of the psalm by David: 'The wicked walk on every side, when the vilest men are exalted.'

Part One

Sugar

MARIA

I

She was a prostitute. Throughout her womanhood all men had been hers and all women had been a challenge to her. She felt herself in a world alienated from that of other women; they seemed to look at her through eyes coloured with hostility. When she got the news of her brother's death in hospital a few weeks past, she wept vehemently, because the people around her felt contented in themselves. She was a cur. Other people rejoiced at what grieved her; they regretted what she liked. Some tried to console her, and some few wept with her, but this made her hate them more. She felt the sting of hypocrisy in their condolences. She remained an outcast, a leper in their moral world. Her unwanted presence was a grain of sand in the eyes. They mourned it. Among the men were those who came to mock her existence, and those who came to her because she was there, because she could serve them. She hated those who came and tried to change her into another kind of a woman, 'a good woman'. She knew she could never change.

A girl on a sofa-bed moved to avoid the rays of the sun which struck her face. She cursed. Maria looked at her, shaking her head worriedly. 'Another whore,' she said to herself. She feared that she was bringing up another prostitute who would take her position when she was dead. The girl looked exactly like her mother. She was the fruit of sin between brother and sister. Maria had sinned with her brother, a sin which grew into a dark spot in their hearts. Nancy was a star in this darkness and her presence glittered, trying to wash out the darkness, but instead exposing it more 'Nancy, it is seven now, aren't you going to school?' Maria asked. She wanted the girl out of her sight. In the presence of her daughter, Maria had a feeling of guilt which nearly drove her mad. Sometimes she wished she could kill Nancy and wipe out her accusing presence. She had tried to kill the baby just after birth but whenever she showed death the prey, it would not respond. One day she had picked up the baby and gone with it to a latrine, but when she tried to drop it into the pit her hands would not let go and she was shaken. She had fallen down and the baby was hurled into a corner of the latrine where it cried wildly.

Now the baby had grown into a girl, she could no longer kill it. The earlier incident had made her suffer a guilty conscience which broke into wild delirium in the night. She had become frightened when her neighbour, Ana, told her that she spoke strange words in the night. She did not want to blurt out things in the darkness again. She could do it by other means, but then she feared those 'other means'.

'She is my daughter, God presented me with her. Why kill her?' There was something which united them both and the urge to kill her seemed like an urge to commit suicide.

'Mama, I am going to school,' Nancy said, as she walked out the door with a bundle of books. Maria looked at the girl through the window as she disappeared amongst the other houses. She envied her daughter's well-built body. 'A good mother-to-be,' she thought.

There was a knock on the door. Maria knew who it was and she dreaded him. The heavy body of a man, bearded or fat-bellied, lame or blind, the stench of sweat mixed with cigarettes. She hated her profession. But there was Nancy, there were clothes to be bought and what-have-you.

Money, and the cheap sale of one's body to get it. The labourious work of twitching one's hips throughout the day, the pains, the heated insides worn out by hourly thrashes, daily thrashes. She feared for her health, feared herself and the type of life she was leading.

She remembered the times a man would come – hot, charging like a bull racing towards grass in the fields – and this man would hand Maria the money and rush her to bed. She had to handle such men to control their wild jerkings, their urges to make her feel pain, otherwise they would hurt her. When she was still new to the profession and a young girl, such men made her whimper or scream. This made them very happy. She marked their faces and never accepted them again. Then she became experienced and such actions made her laugh aloud at the men, mocking them and looking them straight in the eye with derision. They would begin violently and wildly, plunging this way and that, making sure they touched every corner of her body, but after a short time they would sit and soften like jellyfish.

'Come in,' she said, as she sat upon her bed. The door opened slowly and the man walked in quietly, as if there were a serpent he did not want to disturb. He closed the door behind him and stood erect before the woman, his eyes cast shyly towards the ground. Maria looked at him as though questioning who he was and what on earth he wanted in her house. But she said nothing, she just looked at the man who stood there waiting. His shirt was bright white; his trousers, black, with the toes of his shoes peeping from beneath like lizards coming out of a hole.

'Nafasi?' he asked hesitatingly.

'What do you mean', "nafasi"?' Maria asked back rather rudely, but her lips smiled at him.

'I mean, can you serve me?' the man said, now more firmly.

She looked at him from tip to toe, virtually stripping every bit of cloth from his body. She seemed to X-ray him with her eyes. There was no disease. Her eyes rose and looked straight into his and remained fixed there. The man thrust his hand into his pocket and fished out a ten-shilling note. He handed it to her. She took the money and tucked it into her bosom. Then she tried to put the bed into order, but the sheets were too disheveled to be rearranged in a short time.

'Come,' Maria told the man as she lay flat on the bed. The man had already unbuttoned his trousers, the waist band already down to his knees. He went to her. Maria cursed as she washed herself from a bowl. 'It is all shit,' she said to herself, sneering. She wondered how it would have been if she had never been touched, if she were a nun. How would she look? A woman- simple, beautiful and natural. Nobody would have degraded her.

But then, there was her body, used! Money, that was it's name. It was all the wealth she had. If somehow a man came to her and chopped off that which made her a woman, she would starve. Yet there she was, cursing her womanhood, dreading the smells in the room which were nothing but the smells of her trade.

She stood up and walked to the door. The sun outside had already heated up. She gazed upon the busy street. Different types of people stirring like bees in a hive. Some others, beautifully shaped girls of Nancy's age, going in and out of shops. A good number of shabby, tough, ugly-looking men carrying sacks and huge loads on their backs into and out of Indian shops.

'Mami Nancy!' a voice called from outside, through the back door. Maria walked sluggishly to the door, her legs moving lifelessly below her flopping buttocks. She opened the door.

'Come in Mami Joseph,' Maria said as she walked back into the room. The other woman followed, tall and massive. Her fat body seemed to be falling onto her bamboo – shaped legs, her feet sweeping softly on the cement floor.

'You had a man early this morning?' Ana asked knowingly, for the smell in the room, the tousled sheets and the tired look on Maria's face showed it plainly.

'Ah, yes. One of those single-grain birds. They peck a single grain of maize and they are satisfied,' Maria said.

'I like them, you know. They hit once and fast, which doesn't tire you much,' the tall woman rejoined, patting her buttocks as she spoke.

'But some of them are dangerous, they go and chew some herb then come to you stiffer than ebony. Then they will thrash you till you feel like vomiting!' Maria said, and they both laughed loudly as Maria tried to imitate how the man would move about.

'I sometimes enjoy it,' said Ana, 'don't you?'

'No, I don't I don't enjoy it one bit. It is only the money I am after, even if a man came and asked for a thrash on the buttocks, if he gave me a double sum, I would let him!', Maria said, and another burst of laughter followed.

'But they say it is common nowadays. Some of our business mates at Kisulu do it, you know, and they get lots of money.'

'No,' Maria said, 'I just made a joke. Let's not talk about it, it sounds very bestial.'

They remained quiet for some time. Maria looked without expression at the rough bed, unbothered by it. It looked like a jungle where two elephants had been fighting. The couch where Nancy had been sleeping had no cover. The girl had left some books placed carelessly on the small table. Near a corner of the room were dirty teapots, a cooking stove, a cupboard. Flies tried to penetrate through the wire gauze window of the cupboard. They buzzed everywhere, jumping from the bowl Maria had used for washing herself to the teapot, and from there to the bed, to the wire gauze, then back to the bowl.

'I've brought the herbs,' Ana said, producing a bundle of well-wrapped roots and leaves of an herb they called bombo.

'Thank you,' Maria replied to Ana, and smiled with satisfaction.

'You know how to administer them?' Ana asked.

'No.'

'Now, listen,' Ana said, trying to be more serious. Maria moved closer. 'You boil these roots in water mixed with man's urine, then you take some of these leaves, smear them with some semen, then dry them. In the morning, wash yourself in the liquor of boiled roots. And the leaves, put them in fire, letting the smoke fill the house.'

'Are you sure it will work?'

'Sure,' said Ana firmly, 'don't you see my size, my old, ugly look? But men come flocking to me like cows to a stream at noon. Fat-bellied men, teenaged kids and college boys!'

Maria smiled to herself as she put the herbs under the pillow. Ana also smiled.

'I am going,' Ana said, standing up lazily.

'Yes. Business must be hot now,' Maria escorted Ana to the

door. There were two men standing at the door peeping in. Ana grabbed the arm of the one who looked older and he followed her.

'Karibu,' Maria told the other one. They went in.

II

Nancy was late from school. Joseph, the son of her neighbour, reported to Maria that he had seen Nancy go into a house at Livingstone Street. The place he named was not very far from where they stayed, and this relieved some of her worries. Yet there was some uneasiness which haunted her, a fear that there was something wrong somewhere. There was this common talk of town boys beating and raping g schoolgirls. One day Nancy had stormed into the small house breathless. When Maria asked her what was the matter, the girl said that a pack of thugs were after her. Then Maria had gone outside to see who was after her daughter, only to find a group of decently dressed young men, talking and laughing excitedly. Seeing her, the whole mob advanced to her, their arms stretched forward. Maria screamed, rushed back into the house and locked the door.

The youths who had chased Nancy were a group of bhang smokers, a mob composed of school boys, local band musicians, bus conductors and sometimes a few off-duty policemen. They spent most of their evening the outside brothels if they had some money to give the prostitutes, or at the beaches looking for someone to rob. Sometimes they raided shops which were open late. It was believed that policemen supplied them with arms and they used these weapons to commit crimes.

Yet this was not what disturbed Maria so much. From Livingstone Street to her house the streets were always filled with armed policemen. What then did she fear? The time was a quarter to six. What was wrong? The girl was never later from school, nor had she ever been reported to have a deep association with any boy, other than Joseph.

The boy seemed to Maria to be well brought-up. She did not expect anything bad from Joseph's association with her daughter. Still, there was this thing which came into her thoughts but not clarifying itself. It tried to create a commonness between her and her daughter. She dreaded the fact that Nancy was born out of sin between her and her brother, and now this commonness between them!

There was a knock at the door, followed by a giggle. She knew who it was and range boiled within her.

'Who is that?' she asked harshly. No answer nor any kind of reply. Maria walked to the door and opened it wide. There was a young boy, about fifteen, dressed in white shorts and a short-sleeved shirt, his face wearing that silly, boyish smile which could drive one insane, especially in Maria's business.

'What do you want here?' she asked him.

'Nafasi', the boy answered, his face drawing into a nervous smile. Maria kept staring at him, rage flushing her frowning face. The boy was scared. He drew out a ten-shilling note from his small pocket and tried to hand it to Maria. The woman did not take it. She stared at him and shrank. He nervously fished another ten-shilling note from his pocket and made as though to hand both to the woman. She continued to stare, but the mask of rage started to grow faint on her face. The boy smiled, still looking scared. Maria giggled. The boy sighed expectantly. She shook her head. The two notes hung challengingly in front of the woman, and the boy stood backed by them, protected by them, promised by them that he could get what he wanted from this middle aged woman.

In the home area it would be an insult, an abominable act. A young boy, probably a school boy, how could he sleep with her? How did he get the money? She stood there motionless, her big body weighing on her thin, almost lifeless legs. She could feel the hungry stare of the boy and it shook her nerves. The restlessness in his eyes, his youthful shyness, the stubborn gaze upon her massive body stirred her. He was excited, an explosion flared violently in his pants; he pushed his hands into his pockets.

'Please…' Again the hungry look as the boy pleaded helplessly, his voice choking in his throat.

'I haven't any more money' he said, almost crying.

Maria dropped her eyes, her face showing a mixture of pity and humiliation. 'I haven't any more money…' The words drummed in her ears with an accusing rhythm. It was not the boy who was standing before her, it was not his childishly helpless, accusing look that challenged her position. No, it was not. It was money again, in the guise of this youth. Why money? She had no answer.

* * *

That day, seventeen years ago, a man had come to her with the same hungry look on his face. He had offered a big sum of money for a full night. She had hesitated, but the man coaxed her with more money and she agreed. She was then young and the stranger was not much order than she. She was hot and the man liked it, he even promised that he would take her the whole week under any expenses and Maria agreed. It was a gorgeous night. The strange power that the man used to handle her, the tenderness that he offered her, not as a prostitute but as an ordinary girl who could live and be cared for, made her offer herself wholly. She presented all of herself, all of her knowledge of sex to the stranger. He accepted it and gave in return the power, the tenderness.

'What's your name?' Maria had asked at last.

'Josephat,' the stranger answered without hesitation.

'I like your name. I used to have a brother with the same name.'

'Where is he now?' he asked.

'I don't know, I left my home five years ago and have had no contact with that brother ever since. They've forgotten me, I think, my family. I might be dead in their minds now.'

Josephat stayed silent for a while, trying to regain strength to continue with their lovemaking. He caressed the woman and pulled her closer to him. He ran his bearded chin down the cleavage between her breasts and she cried out with pleasure. Josephat engulfed her with his strong arms, absorbing her into his presence and Maria felt good. She felt that at least there was a man who could take her as other women were taken, who didn't take the sex play between them as masturbation. He was not like other men who came, handed her the ten shillings, then pushed her to bed, their desire was not for a woman but for somewhere to dump their lust. He was a man that night and she was a woman.

Then the dreadful morning came. The town buses had started moving on the streets and the night was opening itself towards the day. Maria caught the stranger looking at her as if trying to recall something about her. She looked away, a laugh escaping through her breath. But when the night had fled and the clear day brightened their faces, the stranger asked her, 'What's yours, your name, I mean?'

Maria hesitated; she feared mentioning her name. Why was he so keen on her? She would not tell him. Why should she, after all? Wasn't he just like other prostitutes seekers who offered money and obtained sexual satisfaction? Why should he then demand from her something extra, something that could not help him in any way?

But the sensation came. As the man looked at her waiting for the answer, the pleasure of the night, the tenderness came back, the delight she had felt from him.

'Maria', she answered. The sun's rays shone on her face making it glitter with sweat, for the night had been hot and active.

'Where do you come from?' Josephat asked excitedly.

'Arusha', Maria answered. Some nervousness burned in her voice quivered. A light began to dawn in her memory as she eyed the man thoroughly.

'Which section of the town?' he asked.

'Kibla', came the reply from Maria, and her eyes opened wide.

'Who is your father?' Josephat asked. He was then drawing closer and closer to her, his questions coming out almost unthinkingly.

'Kimaryo…' Maria said, and collapsed on his chest, crying.

'Brother Josephat!' she whimpered. They were still for some minutes, Maria weeping onto his breast, Josephat staring blankly into space. What else, he wondered. They had committed it and it could never be withdrawn. What would everybody think of them if anything resulted from their coming together? He pondered their blood kinship and this awful intimacy between them. She was a cursed woman, she had drawn him into her realm and now there they were, intimate, yet brother and sister.

Who was to blame? Did he not come with money and coax her? When she hesitated, did he not plead, urging her with more money than the usual price? Was he to blame, then? Why did he not look for a better type of woman? Was he shy or lazy? Did he lack somehow in masculinity, so that he could only go with 'public' woman? No, Maria was to blame. Had she not run away from her home and become a prostitute? She had made herself available to him because he had money and was wiling to give it to her in exchange for her nakedness. She was there with other prostitutes; he went there as one goes to a shop. It was a s though he had picked the wrong shirt. Was this reason enough to blame Maria alone? Was it right to go to a prostitute, whatever the conditions? No. both were wrong. Who drove the other into sin? A mystery.

When Maria raised her eyes she met the angry look on Josephat. 'Keep away, you devil,' his face seemed to say. 'Come closer, my brother, forgive me,' she said to herself as she stared back, her own face a confusion of guilt, fear and mortification. The sun shone on her, reflecting her blazing face into his eyes. She looked down.

'Forgive me, Josephat,' she muttered nervously. Her voice tore him away from the emptiness inside his head. Recovering his senses, he pushed her violently to the wall. He cursed and rushed for his clothes. Maria stared at him helplessly, saying nothing. What was she to tell him? Did it mean anything to her? After all, she had been away from her family for years. They had forgotten her. The return of Josephat to her drawn them further apart. Did it matter? They would have been the same distance apart even if this thing had not occurred.

She was a whore and the family had rejected her. The intimacy between her and Josephat just clarified the distance between them. There he was, mad at her, cursing… so what? Let him go and tell everybody that he had sex with his sister if he was that mad. Let him go and tell their mother that he had slept with his sister on one bed. Who would be blamed? She was already a prostitute. What was he?

When Josephat had dressed, he walked out of the room without a word. When he had gone Maria felt that he had forgotten something. She felt some of him in her. She wished he could come back so that they could cleanse themselves before the elder. He never came back, though he left something with her: a big wound.

* * *

A lorry rumbled down the street leaving a huge cloud of smoke trailing in its wake. Scraps of paper flew behind it, drawn by the sweeping wind made as the vehicle went down the dirty street. Maria sighed, leaning on the door as the noises of knocking, empty garbage tins, snoring lorry engines and the whistling of the dusty wind faded. She could still smell the unpleasant odour of diesel oil.

When the cloud of smoke cleared, Maria saw the young boy walking down the street, his head lowered, his hands in his pockets. She gasped and ran to the edge of the street, her long dress sweeping the dust.

'Hey, you! Come! Come back! I'm going to take it...' Maria called him, but the boy walked on, his head lowered desperately. She cursed as she walked back to her house. All the people around had turned their attention to her, surprised. Some young boys shouted at her: 'Malaya, Malaya!, It was a common event in that street, so no one took much notice except the young boys. Anybody born in that street knew the words Mhaya, Malaya, mbwa or papa, all of which meant prostitute, but said with more vehemence and bitterness. Most of the pedestrians on the street, the mature ones, married and unmarried, simply ignored the whole scene. They felt no bitterness because most of the men had gone into these very houses once or twice when they had quarreled with their wives. The prostitutes regarded both the men and their business without concern. To them it was just a way of obtaining money. But older wives hated the prostitutes because they shared their husbands with them, or sometimes the prostitutes because they acquired sexual knowledge from them, they could get them whenever they wanted, whenever they wanted to put out the youthful fires raging in their bodies.

Maria felt the empty stares as she has hastened back to her house. At the door she turned about and surveyed the street again. There was Nancy. She was standing at the corner with a young man, looking at her mother. She seemed to have been there for a long time and might have seen all that was happening. They stared at each other for a few seconds, Maria walked into the house. Her stomach groaned. She was hungry.

'Damn it!' she should have taken the double sum of money from the boy and forget all this rubbish about moral? She cursed herself again, lighting a cigarette. That boy, she thought, so young, he could have done nothing other than pant childishly on her belly for a few seconds and she could have had all that money. Why didn't she just do her job and put memories aside, especially those of Josephat? Didn't that girl born between them feed from the same business? She was schooling; she ate and dressed just as other girls. All the money came from the sale of her mother's body.

Maria sat on the bed smoking quietly. The room was by then completely dark. She was hungry, she needed something to eat. Nancy might also be hungry. She sat there tired, her back itching because she had twitched it all day long. There was another man who was coming to sleep there the whole night. She had accepted the money that morning when she was afraid that business was not going to boost during the day. She hated herself for accepting the money. Nancy was coming, she could hear the soft voice of the girl humming taarab. Maria fumbled for the matchbox as she lifted her body from the bed, which squeaked in relief from the weight. She struck a match and lit the lantern.

Hata taka laingiza
Hilo kapu hilo
Kapu halitachagua
Hilo kapu hilo…

Thus the girl sang as she walked into the room, saying nothing to her mother. The song grated on Maria's nerves but she didn't comment. Instead she walked to the bed and sat down thinking of what she had to cook for supper. Nancy repeated the same song many times. The words of the song meant:

> Even rubbish it accepts,
> That basket,
> The basket never selects,
> That basket…

The lantern glowed on their faces. Nancy was trying to rearrange her heap of books. Maria was busy preparing ugali, the common dish in that part of the city.

'Supper is so late…' Nancy complained, as she sat on the bed that her mother used for business.

'Shut up and please get off the bed!' said Maria, all fired up. The girl made a gesture at her and lay flat on the bed. Maria looked at her frowning. She put down the spoon and moved towards the bed. Nancy rose and darted to the other bed where her mother slept when there was no man to sleep with her.

Maria sonya'd[1] as she walked back to the earthen cooker. They remained silent. Maria set a tray on the floor and put two plates on it. She emptied all the ugali into one plate and covered it with the other one so that the dish remained hot while she prepared some fish.

'Why did you come so late from school?' Maria asked. Nancy did not answer. She was looking into a Drum magazine. She merely raised her eyes, looked at her mother and then returned her eyes to her magazine.

'You heard me, Nancy,' Maria said, putting down the earthen bowl and staring at the girl.

'Yes, Mama,' Nancy giggled.

---

1. Kusonya – to make a sound of contempt, scorn or disapproval, by pushing the tongue against the roof of the mouth; the sound is commonly used in a variety of social situations.

'Answer me and stop giggling!' Maria shouted.

'I went to see a friend of mine.'

'What friend of yours?'

'Deo.'

'Who is Deo?'

'A boy, a friend of mine, he stays down…'

'I have told you many times that I don't want to see you going about with these filthy townboys!'

'He is not filthy,' Nancy countered.

'I have spoken and I don't want to see you with him anymore.'

Nancy winced, but she said nothing. Maria put more charcoal into the cooker and the boiled water in another pot. She took an onion, cut it into small pieces and dropped them into an earthen cooking pan, and then she washed them with a little palm oil. After she had added salt, pepper, and slices of tomato, she squeezed a piece of lime into the pan, and put it on the fire to fry. From the cup board she took two small fish and put them into the pot of boiling water.

'You are still a schoolgirl,' Maria said as she turned the vegetables in the frying pan, 'and you want to get involved into matters which are not of your age. Can't you wait…'

'Now, Mama, I've told you that this boy is not as bad as you think. He works, he earns money…'

'And he gives you money to spoil you,' Maria interrupted accusingly.

'If he does, that is not your matter, he is not spoilt and he can never spoil me. He is a good boy.'

'Stop telling me about the goodness of this satan! All I want is that you stop relations with this wasp.'

Nancy poked out her tongue and turned to her Drum. Maria rushed at the girl and caught her hair, pushing her head back and forth.

'You don't poke your tongue at me!' she said. Nancy screamed. Maria let her go and slapped her on the cheek. The girl fell onto the bed crying wildly.

'You are not going to stop me!' she shouted through her wet lips, 'you a damned whore…'

Maria slapped her, several times. The girl screamed and yelled, 'Malaya ananiuaa'. Then she jumped off the bed and picked up the knife that was lying on a kerosene tin. She whirled to confront her mother, her face curved into a murderous mask.

'You touch me again, I make you bleed!'

Maria sonya'd again, and turned scornfully back to the frying onions, which were almost burnt to charcoal.

There was a rap on the door. Maria looked at Nancy and the girl dropped the knife and walked obediently to the bed that was not used for business. She understood her mother.

'Who is that?' Maria asked, moving nearer to the door.

'Me. The appointment,' the man whispered from outside through an opening in the door.

'Ah!' Maria walked lazily to the door and whispered back, 'Come after half an hour, please.'

'Haya', the man agreed. His heavy footsteps could be heard as he walked away. The room became dead silent except for the sizzling sound of oil as Maria poured hot fish soup into the vegetable pan.

She told Nancy to arrange the food on the tray and when she had finished they sat down and ate amicably. 'A new house,' Maria thought. All the time she had been regarding Nancy as just a child who knew nothing other than eating, going to school and coming back to sleep at home. Now it was different. The girl had reached a critical moment where she knew what she was after, a moment when she understood her surroundings. Maria had a feeling that they were going to part in a short while. She wondered what her daughter would become if she tried to be stubborn and imitate her mother. Or would she get married to that much talked about 'good boy'? But she was schooling! Would the boy stop her from schooling and marry her before they went any further and Nancy got pregnant? How could the boy be interested in a girl who was brought up in a 'whore's house'? Maria was aging and it scared her when she thought that Nancy might turn out like her. She would not be able to help Nancy after such an estrangement. She would die of starvations if Nancy were not there when she became old, for men would no longer come to her. Nancy had been her hope and she had focused all her thoughts about the future on the girl, hoping she could get married and take care of her mother. Maria endured all the high expenses of keeping Nancy in school, expecting her to get a nice job and a nice husband at the end.

Now this intruder was going to spoil all the chances of the girl achieving a better life than the one in which she was being raised! Maria could not stand it. She had to stop Nancy from going with that boy. She must warn Nancy of the fate that awaited them if she chose to go on with him.

When the meal was over, Nancy washed the utensils and her mother prepared the bed for night business. She told Nancy that she would sleep in the other bed. The girl agreed without question. That was the usual procedure. Maria separated the two portions of the room with a bedsheet curtain so that the girl could not see during her meeting with the man. Nancy said good-night to her mother when she had washed the utensils.

'Good-night,' Maria replied and the girl walked to the other bed.

'Nancy,' Maria called.

'Yes, Mama.'

'I shall have a word with you tomorrow. Have you lessons at school tomorrow?'

'No, Mama, it will be Sunday.'

'Then we'll talk.'

'Yes, Mama,' Nancy said and walked to her bed. The man knocked at the door. Maria asked who it was and he whispered that it was 'the appointment'. She let him in.

NANCY

I

She was sixteen. A beautiful, well-shaped girl when she was young, Ana, their neighbour and her mother's friend, used to call her mkewe jumbe, which meant 'wife of a chief'. Many women who came to visit her mother commented on her beauty. She used to hate it when she was still a very young girl because Joseph, the son of Ana, and other boys of his age teased her, calling her mtoto mzuri: beautiful child. And she dreaded it, for they didn't stop there, they stroked her buttocks, grabbed and encircled her with their dusty arms.

Now she no longer hated it. She knew she won adoration in the eyes of many men. One day her friend Rosa had commented, 'You are lucky, Nancy.'

'How?' Nancy asked, knowing what Rosa had meant. She liked people who told her that she was pretty.

'Look at me, with pimples all over my face. Do you think I am going to have a boyfriend?'

'Why not? Aren't you just like other girls? You have equal chances with anyone in this school of winning a good boy for a friend. I am not very different from you!'

'You know you are.' Rosa had remarked sadly. Nancy felt sorry for her, though deep in her heart she felt proud. She knew she surpassed most of her school mates in beauty. She had sometimes used Ambi, a popular skin bleaching cream, to lighten her skin, but one of her schoolmates, older than she, had warned her that it would destroy her smooth, chocolate colour. She stopped and was now using a simple skin oil which she bought cheaply. Another day, a man with a car had stopped her, Rosa and another friend, as they were walking back home from school. The man offered them a lift. They accepted and got into the car. When they were two houses from Nancy's home, Nancy told the man to drop them. 'Do you stay in this dirty part of the city?' the man had asked, fixing his eyes on Nancy.

'Yes,' Nancy answered, biting her thumb. Rosa giggled. 'I must have been mistaken. Anyway, you don't deserve staying here,' the man said, and drove off.

'He wanted us…he wanted you,' Rosa had remarked laughing.

'I am still young. He's old and rich. He has a car and I'm a schoolgirl staying here,' Nancy had lamented. That was a few months before she had met Deo. She had not liked when Rosa had said that the old man was 'after her'. How could she go with an old man? Such men should go with women of her mother's age. Was Rosa joking or was she serious? But the man looked at her in that common way a man eyes a woman when he wants something from her, something concerned with sex. He had looked at her… like other men looked at her mother when they came with the money. Maybe I am not beautiful, she had said to herself, I am just like other girls, only the way I dress makes me appear older.

* * *

Nancy was a student at Jangwani Girls' Secondary School. Many women in that part of town knew her because she liked to talk, and she entered so many people's homes that they nicknamed her 'tiny radio'. Sometimes she went into their houses so frequently that they feared she would delay their business or prevent men from visiting their houses. At these times, they told her to go away.

She spent most of her time studying at the back of her house when she returned from school. Her mother would not let her into the house because that was t he busiest time of the day. A lot of men came with money. As a result Nancy was always up-to-date with her school work. She was also more gregarious because, when reading bored her, she would take refuge in neighbouring houses and talk there.

Sometimes she would go for a walk with Joseph in the streets. Such moments were rare and very exhilarating to her because she never dared to go into the city alone. Joseph would take her to the beaches and all around, through the busiest streets of Dar es Salaam. Joseph did not like those walks, so he resisted Nancy's pleadings. He yielded only when Nancy came close to tears.

She feared town boys. One day as she sat behind her house, two town boys had approached her. Both were as tall as Joseph. Their faces wore the savage stare of bhang smokers. Nancy had gasped and grabbed her books, trying to take flight to her home. But one of them caught her arm, so that when she let go, all her books flew into the drainage ditch which passed near the house. Nancy had screamed, but the other boy put his palm on her mouth as he tried to tear down her knickers. Nancy kicked this way and that, trying to keep the second boy away from her.

'Don't play it cool, boy, fix her legs and go in fast,' the first boy said as he squeezed her arms, pulling closer and putting her into position for the other boy. Nancy had struggled hard, but the first boy was too strong for her.

'Keep cool, baby,' said the second boy as he unzipped his pants. 'It doesn't hurt.'

'Quick, I'm waiting,' the first one said. When the second prepared to move on Nancy, another boy came from behind and landed an iron bar on his back. The two assailants ran away, leaving Nancy with her rescuer. She turned to see that it was Joseph.

Nancy liked Joseph. They were age-mates but the boy had learnt so many things from the city that he was by far her superior in maturity. He taught her many things.

Whenever he had passed an event in town he would come home and narrate it to Nancy, who always appreciated everything that happened in town.

'Let's do it,' Nancy said to Joseph one day.

'What?' Joseph asked.

'You know, I have always wanted to do it.'

'What?' asked Joseph, and Nancy, failing to pronounce the words, moved to him and clutched him, drawing their bellies closer. She was twelve years old at the time.

'Oh! You have never done it?' Joseph had asked.

'No.'

'I'll show you. Come this way,' Joseph said and led her to a corner behind his house. He told her to lie down. Nancy had liked the game. Joseph had been the teacher. As time went on Nancy found other friends who wanted to do the same thing. Nancy and Joseph parted, and she went on with other boys. She didn't have many, though, and the 'game' always ended before it was complete. They feared her, the boys, maybe because she was beautiful.

* * *

The morning after their quarrel over Deo, Nancy's mother was very bitter about it. Nancy always remembered her words; the painful appeal held in the words made her hate them, and she also feared them. She tried to forget what her mother had said and carry on her friendship with Deo.

'You are a schoolgirl, Nancy,' Maria had said to her. "You are my daughter. But last night I came to realize that you have just become another woman. Your breasts are now full and you have come to feel that we can face each other, talk to each other as two women, now that you can walk alone in the street and do things according to your own wishes.

I am your mother, I have known the world and felt its bitterness. I know, Nancy, you have reached a critical age for a girl and you have discovered what boys are. Yesterday you were late from school and you said that you had this boy, Deo, the "good boy". You showed protest when I told you to leave him alone, which means you have a feeling that you are now able to distinguish the bad from the good. Alright.

Now I am saying that I will not stop you from these activities of yours. But you should realize that you have not reached an age right for marriage. That you are schooling and have to pass your days in school peacefully. I don't walk you to school, I am not there where you spend most of your daytime and I can see that I cannot draw a line between you and the world. I have to let you into it sooner or later. But I am making this motherly appeal to you. I am working hard to make us survive, to bring you up and let you realize that this life we are living is not the right one for human beings. You have seen well-brought up girls at your school, you have seen many things which they have, and that you haven't. Ours is a bad home. Who is to blame but fate? I love you, my daughter, that is why

I am struggling and working hard to keep you up and prepare a good future for both of us. We are not a bad lot, as many of the people think. We are working hard and earning money, which is what everybody is after...'

She moved to her daughter, held her tight and said 'Nancy, do listen to me, we have no money – we need it, we would be dead without it. I am working hard and you are my only hope. I don't want you to end in the same suffering, because nobody will value you after that. I want you to be a good daughter and one day a good mother.

'So when you go along with these friends of yours, beware of those who will spoil you. Know the right friend and the wrong one. Some of your girlfriends might be the ones who can spoil you. The men, most of them will try to drag you off the right track without your knowledge. I know it may happen, it will, and it will be because you are still young and new to the world, you have not yet discovered it and you have to be introduced to it slowly. I know it, I have seen it, listen to me. When you go about with these men, think of these words, think of me...'

And they sat there on the sofa silently. Nancy, her face sullen and dark, leaned to support herself on a chair beside the sofa. She was breathing fast, holding her tears within her breast. Her mother had lit a cigarette and was softly blowing the smoke towards the ceiling. The air was heavy and hot as the charcoal in the earthen cooker glowing brightly, burning off a few remaining chips of wood.

Outside there was a drizzle, the people had vacated the nearby market place and gone back to their homes. There remained an empty quietness except for the occasional automobiles roaring down the wet tarmac.

II

Deo sat on a wooden coach at Uhuru Gardens waiting for Nancy. A handsome, tall youth, skinny and almost shy, he dressed smartly and combed his hair into a huge nest over his head. The tight shirt and the platform shoes which he wore made him appear ghostly tall. Today he was red all over: red shirt, red bell-bottomed trousers and brown shoes.

Deo was working at Mountain Goat Rubber Factory. After Form Six at Mkwawa High School, the boy had been sponsored by the factory to go and study the rubber industry in Ceylon. He came back after one year and was placed in the laboratory of the factory. He was in his early twenties. He had met Nancy just a few months after his return from abroad.

It had been a school day, when classes were over. Rosa and Nancy were talking in high pitches as they walked up Livingstone Street. Deo was walking quickly ahead of them, but when he heard the two girls giggling behind him he slowed down to let them pass. The girls walked fast and overtook him. Nancy's shoulder brushed against him as they passed. When they had moved a few metres ahead of him, they, too, slowed down. Deo, enjoying the game, went on and rubbed his shoulder against Nancy. A few paces later, he slowed down and the girls closed the distance.

'Good morning, ndugu,' Nancy said. It was afternoon.

'Good-night,' Deo answered. Rosa giggled.

'Good afternoon, then,' Nancy said, laughing lightly.

'I said good-night, didn't you hear?' The boy said smiling.

After a swift exchange of banter the three introduced themselves. Deo concentrated his talk on Nancy, so Rosa quickened her pace and left them behind '…that does not matter,' Nancy had said as they approached her home, 'I am a schoolgirl, yes, but my schooling does not interfere with this.'

'No, it doesn't,' Deo said, 'but I hope you know how much one pays after making a schoolgirl pregnant.'

'Does that bother you? How many girls in this city are running about with boys but are not pregnant? You are not such a maniac about that thing, I hope,' Nancy said, laughing shyly.

Deo had asked then, that day, for her to be his girlfriend, his partner, and it pleased Nancy very much. They stood at the entrance of the house for a long time, talking. It was six o'clock. Nancy wanted to leave. She said to Deo, 'You would not be very pleased to know where I live, I know this. But I want you to know it as early as now.'

'I would be glad to know the place,' Deo said and the girl took him up the street till they were just a few metres from her home.

'There,' Nancy told him, pointing to the house. The boy sucked in his breath quickly, covering his mouth with his hand. He knew that place!

'You have been here before?' she asked, careful to let her face show no expression.

The boy shook his head, sighing. 'No, but it's hard to believe.'

'Believe it then,' Nancy said, looking away desperately. The boy came closer to her and embraced her.

'I knew it,' Nancy said tearfully, 'you are not going to have me as your girlfriend because I am from that house. I knew it…'

'No, Nancy, you don't know,' Deo said as he kissed her lightly, gently. 'Beautiful shirts may miss a button.'

A few weeks went by. Deo wondered, as he remembered that first day, why he had fallen in love with a whore's daughter. The girl was beautiful, but wasn't she after money just like her mother? He never stopped wondering how such a beautiful girl could be born in a prostitute's house.

* * *

A long vehicle hooted at the bus stop, jolting Deo from his musing. Some passengers jumped out and walked away hastily. There was an old man with a middle-aged woman. The man rounded his arm on her hips as they walked away from the bus stop. Nobody took note of it but Deo; behind them was Nancy. She was dressed in the new, red, bell-bottomed slacks which Deo had bought for her a week ago, and she wore a white blouse. Her hair was plaited into a pattern, with the end of her plaits hanging over both ears like buffalo horns. The broad-bottomed pants swept over the grass as she moved gaily across the garden towards Deo.

'Am I very late?' she asked as she sat close to Deo on the wooden bench. He wrinkled his forehead as if in anger, then looked straight into her face. She blinked and lowered her eyes.

'Not very,' he said, relaxing his face. She sighed. The boy looked at her, chuckling softly. He put his left arm across her lap and leaned towards her.

'Do I frighten you?' he asked, smiling. He had a small gap between his two front teeth. She did not look up.

'Not you,' she said, also smiling, 'I am not scared by people of your type. You are always harmless.'

'Damn it!' He pronounced the words the way Afro-Americans do. 'People of my type are first-class rapists,' he said, returning to their own language.

'Ha!' Nancy snapped. 'Can you imagine such a smartly dressed young man, soft and gentle, doing such a horrid act?'

'Why not?' he said in English.

'No,' she said, her white teeth fully exposed, 'rapists are a penniless, shabbily dressed lot. They are jobless and always hungry for women and food, they are respected by no one, they are frustrated by their surroundings, they sink into smoking bhang, stealing, and raping.'

'Hey! You have quite a good knowledge of them!' Deo happily encircled her with his long arms.

A cool, soft breeze blew on their faces as it swept across the garden. The leaves of the young coconut palm over their bench swung in harmony with the wind. It was a quarter past six and the faint rays of the setting sun washed the horizon red. The clear sky promised a peaceful evening as it capped the big city with empty blue. They sat kissing, unaware of their surroundings, unaware of the city, so busy and noisy. Nancy felt peacefulness, coming from nowhere in particular; it engulfed her in a strange world. She was apprehensive but she felt good. Her body seemed to be floating on a bizarre level of consciousness which she had never before experienced. He held her closer, and the distant, endless roar of the city went on around them, unable to intrude on their exuberant possessiveness.

The garden was quiet as the evening drew its dark curtain over the city. Lights blinked on and soft music from a bar at the center of the garden raised them from their dreamy world. Deo sat up quickly.

'We are late,' he said. 'The film starts at a quarter to seven and it is now twenty minutes to.'

'Oh!'

'Let's go, then,' he said, pulling her up, 'we'll take a cab.' They walked swiftly along the lane, crossing the garden towards a taxi stand. At the stand was an ancient Mercedes Benz, two Ford Cortinas and a Zephyr. They took the Zephyr.

'Empress Cinema, please,' Deo told the taxi driver, who immediately slammed his door and switched on the engine. He swerved the car in an about-turn and let it slide into the street. As he accelerated the Zephyr slid softly down Uhuru Street.

'Faster, please. We have an appointment,' Deo said. 'O.K.,' said the driver, and he pumped more fuel into the chamber.

A cool evening wind whistled through the windows as the car sped through the tarmacked streets. In the momentary silence of the car Nancy's mind flashed back to her mother at home. She must have a lot of customers now. Nancy had been seen with Deo several times by her mother after the warning she had given her. Maria did not say anything; she knew Nancy had already decided, and blocking her way would only make the girl run away to start a wilder life.

'I will be going out, Mama,' Nancy had said that morning.

'When?' Maria had asked.

'This evening, with Deo.'

'Where are you going?'

'To a cinema. But I will be back early.'

'Think it over yourself. When you have decided you can go or stay.'

Maria had appeared unconcerned. Nancy liked the new attitude because it meant freedom to her, though it gave her the full burden of responsibility. She had decided to go, and when the evening approached she put on her brightest clothing. She went over to her mother and said, 'Mama, I am going.'

'Haa! Nancy!' Maria had exclaimed. 'Where did you buy these expensive clothes?'

'At Tee Kay's, Mama. Deo bought them for me,' Nancy said, moving into the light for her mother to see.

'He is a good friend, this Deo,' Maria said, smiling.

'Yes, Mama. He likes me very much.'

'And has money.'

'Yes, he works, Mama, I told you that day.'

There followed a long silence. Nancy stared down at her mother, who was sitting on a stool. She appeared aged and exhausted. Nancy wished she could pull her up, mould her into a beautiful girl and go with her to meet Deo. But the woman sat there, old and destroyed by her profession. She stared into the street with a veteran's simplicity, waiting for money for men.

'Mama, I am going,' Nancy said.

'Yes, go, but watch that Deo of yours, see that you don't run into trouble with him.'

Nancy did not hear the last words because she had already left.

* * *

The taxi came to a halt. Deo paid the fare and the car moved away. He took Nancy's arm and walked her along a corridor till they came to the ticket chamber.

'Wait here, I'm going to buy the tickets,' he said.

'Yes,' she answered nervously. It was the first time she had attended a film show. She wondered how marvelous or how bad it would be. She studied the huge pictures on the walls. There was the biggest of them all, facing her from the opposite wall. It was the face of a Japanese or Chinese man. On top of the picture was a large heading: The Big Boss, and below the picture was a name: Bruce Lee. The other pictures had the same heading, only they lacked the name at the bottom.

'Let's go this way,' Deo said, grabbing her arm. 'We are almost late.' They went up the steps through the back door-curtain. The ticket collector showed them their seats and they sat down. The screen was painted: Intermission and lights went on.

'You will enjoy it, I tell you,' Deo said. 'It is about Kung Fu fighting. This is the second time I am seeing it.'

'Oh.'

'That Bruce Lee is a pretty good fighter. I like him.'

'Hmmnn.'

'Oh, yes. He can beat ten people in a minute.'

'Ah!'

Nancy did not want to talk much. She didn't want people t o know that it was her first time to go to a film show. She listened, and Deo talked. After the intermission he talked less; he fixed his eyes on the screen, almost unaware of her presence. She too, was occupied by the film.

'It was wonderful!' Nancy exclaimed after the show, as they walked towards a bus stop.

'I knew you'd like it,' said Deo as he squeezed her hand tight. A bus hooted before them at the stop. It bore the label: KARIAKOO. They embarked and took a double seat. At that hour, the bus was almost empty and the conductor came straight to them after pressing the bell button. Deo paid for double fare.

At Mnazi Mmoja the bus stopped and dropped them. They crossed Uhuru Street, waked a few metres until they came to Livingtstone. They did not talk. At the door of her home, Nancy kissed him good-night.

'Come with Rosa on Sunday, we shall prepare something special for you.'

'When? I mean at what time?'.

'Hmmm… make it at ten in the morning.'

'I shall try. Will there be two of you?'

'Yes, Frank will be with me the whole day.'

'O.K,' she said and Deo held onto her hand so tightly, until she let out a little cry. They parted and Nancy gave a slight push on the door. It opened. She tiptoed in, closing it behind her. There was a man! She could hear a bed squeaking and the strong breathing of the man. 'Business,' she said to herself and sneaked to the other bed. Her mother did not say a word.

III

Sunday came. The morning was bright and warm, cheered with the usual Sunday bells and Christian choir on the radio. There were few cars in the street but lorries, in their usual routine, kept moving about in an undisturbed, irritating roar. There were people on the streets, but most of them were the never-miss, rugged dock boys, construction apprentices, and street sweepers who were walking to their jobs. Following the usual daily procedure, the sidewalk was covered by simple tradesmen and women selling various articles: foodstuffs, cosmetics, cooking utensils and so on.

'You are not going to church, Maria?' asked Ana, more or less making a commentary. She was peeping through the half open door. Nancy sat up on the sofa bed. The sun beamed straight into her eyes. She sonya'd and covered her eyes with her hands. Her mother lay flat on the bed on which a man was never allowed to lie.

'Oh, no. I never go there. Only big men go because they have a better chance to be more Christian than all of us.'

'I am going,' Ana said, 'I have decided to try it today.' Maria laughed her loudly. Nancy giggled.

'Hehe…ehhe…heh. You will be committing more sin by going there than by staying in your shanty.'

'Why?' asked Ana, annoyed.

'They are not going to appreciate your presence even if you are going to confess your sins. I tell you, believe me. They are going to stare at you with their fat, accusing eyes, forgetting that you have once or twice slept with most of them.' Nancy walked to the cupboard. She took the teapot, went with it to a water tap outside, washed it, filled it with water and returned to put it on the charcoal cooker.

'I am going,' Ana declared.

'To church?' Maria asked.

'No back to my shanty. There might be some business.' Nancy giggled and Maria broke into wild laughter.

'Yes, Maria agreed, 'you'd better go and obtain some few coins.' Nancy smiled to herself as she watched the tall, massive woman disappear at the door. 'Cursed lot,' her mother had called them one day when she was arguing with a colleague, a woman who stayed a few houses away from theirs. Nancy was outside washing her school uniforms as the two women argued inside. But again Maria had defended herself, '…it is a business, not a courtship, not a sexual relationship.' Did they differ? What was a courtship and what was that game which they did with the customers after taking their money? She brushed away the thought, but another one came: 'Big men have a better chance of becoming better Christians.' Why did she say that? Wasn't Christianity consolation for people's grievances? Wasn't Jesus a saviour? Nancy had gone to church only a few times but these questions made her think that she might have heard the preacher wrong. Maybe Christ was for the chosen few, the Jews, the big men- a selection by Jesus?

The pot boiled. Nancy took a kettle from the cupboard and emptied the boiling tea into it. She put both the tea pot and the kettle into the cupboard, then knotted her khanga tightly round her breasts. After covering her upper body with a second khanga, she took a fifty shilling coin and went to buy buns from the women on the sidewalk.

* * *

Nancy took a bath and unplaited her hair, which she then combed into an Afro style. She took her breakfast and spared some for her mother. Rosa would soon be coming. She did not want to dress until she saw what Rosa had put on. She heard the church service programme playing on all the radios of the neighbours. The services usually started at nine, so she took it to be a few minutes after nine. She cut her finger-nails short and then oiled her face. She wiped most of this off with a khanga, and plastered the rest with a grey powder. She then wiped most of the concoction off so that she mighty not appear ridiculously light.

'Hodi?' called a voice at the door.

'Karibu', Nancy answered. Rosa walked in after closing the door.

'Haa, Rosa!' Nancy exclaimed as she stood up to welcome her friend. They hailed each other, their palms connecting in a loud clap.

'I didn't know you would be so early!' Nancy said, almost shouting.

'Am I? I thought I would find you gone'.

'Heee! You don't know how I drag along'.

'Ah, no. I know you. Not when you have an appointment,' Rosa said and they broke into brisk laughter. Nancy went behind the bedsheet curtain and dressed. Rosa waited. She, too, had combed her hair into a nice, round bush. As she sat on a short stool, her long pink maxi-skirt spread itself on the cemented floor. She pulled it up and piled the heap of bright cloth on her knees.

Nancy came out wearing a blue maxi-skirt adorned with black and green rings. Like her friend, she sported a white blouse. Rosa stood up and walked to the door. Nancy peeped through the curtain and said in a whisper, 'Mama, we are going'.

'Yes,' Maria said, 'will you be in for lunch?'

'I think we won't.'

'As you please,' the mother said lazily and turned over in her bed to face the wall. The girls walked out and crossed the street parallel to the house, then they turned up sandy Kondoa Street.

'Eh, Rosa, I didn't tell you about that film show,' Nancy said as they trotted on the sand, their bodies bent forward to maintain their balance.

'Which film show?' Rosa asked.

'Have you forgotten that date I had with Deo on Friday?' Nancy asked, stopping to eye Rosa with a mocking smile.

'Ah, yes, did you go to a film show?'

'Oh, yes, and it was beautiful.'

'What was it about?' Rosa asked enviously.

'A certain Kung-fu fighting Chinese.'

'Hmmm.'

'Against a certain Big Boss.'

'Only those?'

'Yes. The Big Boss had thugs and lots of money. The fighter had the energy to beat up all the thugs and proved the impotence of the Big Boss' money.'

'I fear films in which people fight, they make me dream about them at night.'

'Do you? I didn't know you were such a coward.'
Nancy remarked with feigned annoyance.

'I'm telling you!'

'Then you are unlucky. I liked everything in that film. The beautiful girl was so vulnerable and appealing that the fighter appeared as a complete hero. I wish I could do the same.'

'Deo is not a fighter,' Rosa said, laughing.

Nancy frowned a little. 'Nobody fights in that manner in Dar es Salaam, but there are other hot fights where he stands up well and shows himself to be tough.'

'For example?'

'Em… em…girls.'

'How? In that case you will be the fighter, with your beauty.'

'Ah, yes,' Nancy rejoined. She chose to deliberately misinterpret Rosa's remark.

You are right! Deo will be the beauty and I will be the fighter holding him from other girls!'

'And you have that potential Nancy, I tell you.'

'What flattery!' Nancy said, and they both laughed.

* * *

At Deo's door they pause outside, peeped in and listened.

'I wish these women could stop this crap about their so-called emancipation and start first with clearing up their own ills,' an unfamiliar voice commented.

'Hmmnh?'

'It is to raw to stomach, this stuff. They talk and talk and talk. You would think they want to exchange what they have got for balls! Sometimes, Deo, I think they are mad.'

'Aren't they?' The familiar voice of Deo spoke, and the girls were pleased. Nancy wanted to knock on the door but Rosa, with a silly laugh, pulled her hand away.

'See, Deo, the women have kept quiet for many years and now their tongues have loosened, they have been activated. They want to say something, at least, but they fail to pick the right themes.'

'You are right.' Again it was Deo. Nancy moved and knocked on the door. Rosa hugged her nervously. They giggled.

'Hodi!' Nancy called at the door.

'Karibu,' the strange voice answered from inside. The girls did not go in. They heard footsteps coming from inside which made them crowd to one side of the door, giggling.

'So, it is you,' Deo said after opening the door. 'Come in, we don't keep tigers in here.'

They followed him into the sitting room. Inside was the other young man. He was learning over a newspaper when the girls walked in. When Deo had asked them to be seated, the other youth raised his eyes, gave a smile and saluted them. 'Good Sunday to you all.'

'Asante,' the girls said, smiling back.

'Frank, meet Rosa and Nancy. And Rosa, Nancy, this is Frank, my good friend.'

They shook hands. Deo disappeared into another room. Frank went over to the record player and picked his favourite numbers. He piled the records on the automatic player and switched it on, then sat down again.

'What a day,' Nancy thought. The music floated from the stereo speakers into their ears, filtered by the warm air. Deo came back with four glasses, two beer bottles and two medium-size Martini bottles. He put the tray on a table and set a drink for each of them on four short stools.

'Is it strong?' Nancy asked when he served her a martini.

'Not at all,' Deo assured her, opening his own beer bottle. 'The softest of all foreign drinks.'

Nancy sipped the warm vermouth. 'Watch out you don't run into trouble with this Deo of yours.' Her mother's remark scared her. She never drank. What would Mama say if she saw her drinking? 'As you please?' Or would she say, 'Remember my words..?' But I am young, Nancy thought, one has to do these things during one's youth nowadays. My mother grew up in an age when no boys spent money on girls. But how did she become a prostitute? Why did she decide upon that way of making money? Why was she not married? How was she, Nancy, born? The questions grew and multiplied into an argument in her head, exposing the truth of her own existence.

'You don't seem to like its taste, Nancy,' Frank said. 'I'd better bring you some lemon juice to sweeten it.'

'Yes, please,' Nancy said absently. Frank disappeared into the other room and came back with a bottle of lemon juice.

When the girls had drained two glasses of the stuff, Nancy started to feel dizzy. It was noon and the room became hotter. Frank and Deo were dancing. At first she was not impressed by their movements; she looked at them with mild derision. Now the dizziness overpowered her and she felt the urge to stand up and brush it off with movements. She felt guilty for accepting the alcohol. Rosa appeared even more drunk. She sat on the sofa, carelessly flexing her legs and sometimes twitching her hips, following the tune of the music. She laughed easily when Frank gestured to her, but refused when he asked her to dance.

'Deo,' Nancy called softly, with her head bowed and her hand on the stool trying to write something.

'Yes, please,' He leaned and kissed her brow.

'Ah…' She backed away.

'Oho, now don't say I was going to bite you,' he said, looking at her with a tipsy grin.

'Where is the toilet, please?' Nancy asked.

She walked out with Deo, leaving the other two in room. When they came back, Rosa and Frank were dancing. Rosa sank her head onto Frank's broad chest, and the latter made a 'V' with his arms on her back, his palms resting on her buttocks. Nancy went to her seat and took gulps of martini without lemon juice. Deo came to her, swaying. He and Frank had been emptying beer bottles one after another into their stomachs. They were drunk and the girls, too, were drunk. He bowed to Nancy and she stood up. They swayed on the floor with movements which did not match. Rosa and Frank went to the toilet.

After half an hour, again Nancy was escorted to the toilet by Deo. She swayed, and her eyes rolled prettily under their lids, looking at him as he carried her in a half-embrace. They trotted down the steps, all her weight supported on his shoulder, laughing as they swept their feet on the earth like donkeys in the desert.

The room was empty when they came back. The record player was still on and the number was Tabu Lay's 'Mongali.' Deo locked the main door with a key, then turned to Nancy to request a dance.

'Where are the others?' she asked, fright in her eyes.

'You can guess,' Deo said, stretching his long arms to her.

'No, not until you tell me where Rosa has gone.'

'Come on, let's dance.'

'No! Where is Rosa?' she persisted weakly, backing away from him.

'O.K. I'll show you.'

They went into the bedroom. Another soft tune filled the empty room as they left: 'Killing Me Softly with His Song.'

IV

Nancy was not exceptionally bright in school, but her earlier school reports had shown that she could go on with studies after Form Four. She was hard-working. She did all the homework she was given at school. This was because all her time after school was spent outside her home, waiting for her mother to earn their money. Nancy studied and she let no class notes go unrevised; that was the only way she could keep herself busy. Miss Barefoot, the English teacher, who was from Ireland, liked Nancy because she was very good at spoken and written English. Sometimes Miss Barefoot invited the girl to her home for a cup of coffee. They talked about all sorts of things. The teacher would ask Nancy about 'life in the villages,' but Nancy really did not know anything about it, and she told the woman so. When the teacher asked her about life in Dar es Salaam, Nancy could only speak of the bad women, thugs, and the infrequent entertainment she had had; most of the latter was lies. The girl did not say that her mother was a prostitute.

It was March. They were doing their Form Four leaving examination in November. That Monday, Miss Barefoot asked Nancy to come to her apartment for a cup of tea. Nancy agreed, very excited. She would have a lot to tell her teacher about the week-end and bout the film show she had seen with Deo. As Nancy sat in the last class that day, her mind was much occupied with thoughts of Deo; she grasped nothing of what the biology teacher was saying.

She took no notes as she sat in the back row. The burden of learning only seemed to get in the way of her wishful thinking about Deo.

* * *

Rosa had not come to school that day. She had awakened with a serious headache. Her hangover from Sunday beat with an itching irritation inside her head. Nancy had gone by to collect her that morning for school, only to meet the cold, angry look of Rosa's mother. She told Nancy flatly that Rosa would not be going to school with her that day. Nancy had not asked why. She turned away and walked towards school, annoyed.

'Do I care?' Nancy had thought. 'Did I blow the alcohol into her mouth? If she thinks I am going to destroy her daughter, why didn't she stop her from going around with me at the start?' Nancy smiled when she remembered that Sunday, walking with Deo into the bedroom and finding Frank holding Rosa, his eyes shut. As he jerked back and forth, his teeth had ground on each other like a saw cutting soft wood.

It was wild, it was not the same as when her mother did it, in secrecy. Why had they done it that way?'

A piece of chalk hit Nancy. She looked up and found the old teacher, Mr Kirkby, staring at her. She lowered her face shyly and picked up a pen from the desk

'Why aren't you taking notes, Nancy?' the teacher asked. She did not answer, but started scribbling on the open exercise book. There was no point to note, so she copied words from the blackboard, even though she did not understand their meaning. Kirkby picked up his books and walked out. Nancy followed behind, as the period was over.

* * *

Miss Barefoot was reading the Daily News when Nancy pressed the door bell.

'Oh, Nancy!' she said, smiling as she opened the door. They went in together to the sitting room. Miss Barefoot gave Nancy the paper and went into the kitchen. She came back with a tea tray.

'Your report has not been very pleasing in the last two months,

Nancy,' Miss Barefoot said, after they had remained silent for some time. Nancy made no comment, she only looked at the carpet with a mortified smile.

'You know, Nancy, this is the toughest year for you.'

'But Miss Barefoot, we have not done any exams,' she protested.

'I know. But I don't want you to get involved when you are studying for your exams.' The woman's face was serious.

'I am not involved. Miss Barefoot.'

"That is why I am telling you this is your toughest year. I can see you are at a critical age for a schoolgirl. You have to have more of a sense of responsibility whenever you are doing anything. You have your exams that should be the foremost thing.'

'Yes, Miss Barefoot,' Nancy said, relaxing. They both sipped their tea.

'I am telling you this as a friend, not as your teacher. I want you to be what I once wished to be, a barrister.'

Another long silence followed. Nancy bit her toast and munched, waiting for more words from the teacher. The woman said nothing more.

After the tea, Miss Barefoot asked, 'How was the weekend?'

'Not bad. I was just at home reading Things Fall Apart.'

'Oh. Is that your English literature textbook?'

'Yes, Miss Barefoot.'

'Do you like it?'

'It is very good.'

'Better than A Man For All Seasons?'

'No,' Nancy said, and the teacher laughed. Another silence. Miss Barefoot lit a cigarette and smoked quietly, her eyes gazing upon the ceiling. Nancy simply could not tell her about the weekend she had with Deo.

'I am going, Miss Barefoot,' Nancy said, picking up her books from a small table at the center of the room.

'Oh, alright. In fact I was going for some shopping in town. Let's go, I'll give you a lift.'

She drove Nancy to a place along Livingstone Street not very far from her home, and dropped her.

SUGAR ON THE STREETS

I

That Saturday Nancy was walking home from school alone. Rosa had an appointment with Frank and had gone to meet him early, before lessons were over. Thoughts of Deo had been running through Nancy's head that whole week. His image occupied her mind, invincible against any other intruding thought. She wanted to brush the image away, but when she tried to do so, it gave a long, lively smile that melted her. 'He is my first boyfriend. Is Rosa as much affected by Frank as I am by Deo?' she wondered childishly. She walked in long strides, following her path by dint of mere habit.

Abruptly all the images drifted away from her head. As she walked along Maktaba Street, her pace slowed and her stride weakened. She felt limp, her body weighing heavily on her legs. Tiredness overpowered her; she stopped walking for a moment. Her eyes saw only blurred, dark shapes as she staggered to a nearby bus stop and sat down. She was hungry. That morning she did not eat breakfast, and the previous evening she had eaten very little. Dizziness swept over her, and for a full five minutes she leaned slackly against the pole which supported the roofing of the bus stop. She was alone, few people passed, appearing only as dark shapes as she staggered to a nearby bus stop and sat down. Rays of the noontime sun drilled through the corrugated iron sheet cover of the bus stop. For almost fifteen minutes nobody came. Then, when the dizziness had almost vanished, she saw a car coming along the way she had passed. It was a Mercedes Benz. The three-pointed metal star on the head of the car sparkled in the sunshine. Fifty metres away, the car slowed down, sliding softly on the road. It came to a halt in front of her. A very mature man poked out his head and said, 'Where are you going?'

'Livingstone Street,' she said with some hesitation.

'Let's go, I'll give you a lift,' the man replied and he opened the left front door.

'Come this way,' he directed Nancy to the door of the car. She sank into the seat and the man pulled the door shut for her. They drove off. Her dizziness had disappeared but Nancy still felt weak.

'Where are you schooling?' the man asked her.

'Jangwani.'

'Hmmmm.'

He drove silently for some minutes, two or three, then he took a glimpse at her, smiled and said, 'You were so tired when I picked you up.'

'Yes,' Nancy said bashfully, 'it was the sun. It is so hot.'

'Oh, this sun is baking people, damn it,' he agreed.

She did not comment; she was too hungry.

'You must be thirsty now,' he said.

'Yes, but we are not far from my home now.'

At the roundabout that joined Maktaba Street with Livingstone Street the man swerved the Benz into Uhuru Street, the opposite direction from Nancy's home. She raised her head a bit higher and saw where the car was heading.

'But ... I ... I am going to Livingstone Street,' she stammered.

'I know, I know. I have a box of soap to pick up at that shop.' He pointed to a shop a little ahead of them. They came to the shop and he braked the car. He got out, slamming the door. After a minute or two he came back empty-handed.

'Ah, these Indians, they'll always keep you waiting. See, they told me to pick it up tomorrow. It's no problem anyway. One thing: I think you need a cold drink, you must be dying of thirst now.'

Nancy did not answer, she merely smiled shyly. The man released the hand brake, started the engine and off they went down Uhuru Street. Nancy sighed heavily. The man smiled at her.

'How do you like schooling?' he asked after a pause.

'It's fine,' Nancy answered.

'I know most of you take it as a burden.'

'Yes, in some cases. You know the problems of studying.'

'Ah, yes. I used to hate school because I had no money.

My father refused me money because I did not go to boarding school. I stayed at home.'

'Yes. Nowadays it is a big problem to many of us, compared to your times when you could buy lunch with one shilling… or so I have heard!'

'Is that so? So you are in more trouble, schooling, than I was.'

'In that case, yes.' This time Nancy smiled broadly, but she was still wary. The Benz halted at a popular restaurant in town. He got out quickly, opening the door for Nancy and locking it after her. They went into the restaurant.

'My name is Magege,' he whispered into her ear as they walked in.

'Asante. I am Nancy,' she replied, without thinking. She was too excited to really think about what was happening.

'You must be hungry, too,' he said. Nancy made no reply, only an abashed smile. They had occupied a table in a corner at the end of the room.

'May I tick the card for you?' the man asked. Nancy nodded. He ticked two cards and gave them to the waiter. The restaurant was a broad dining room. The soft hum of Indian music mingled with the low voices of people talking and the scratching of flatware on enamel plates. Nancy turned her eyes this way and that exploring the room. There were many types of people, old and young, white and black. She was the only schoolgirl to be seen; her uniform betrayed her. All the other people were dressed nicely in a profusion of colours and styles. The annoying difference between them and her made her restless. All eyes seemed to land on her inferior, blushing presence.

The waiter came with a big tray and laid their plates on the table, drinks in small, corked bottles, and two empty glasses. He then went and brought two water glasses. The labels on the bottles read brandy, whisky, and Coca-cola.

'Help yourself, please,' the man said. She did not move. He pulled one plate to himself and pushed the other to the girl. He uncorked the brandy, filled his own glass then pushed the little whisky bottle toward her. She protested.

'You don't drink?' he asked.

'No, I am a schoolgirl,' she defended herself.

The man took her glass, filled it half with Coca-cola and then up to the brim with whisky. Nancy protested but the man grinned as he said, 'This is softer than the other one; it will make you a bit high, though.'

Nancy shuddered. She did not want to go home swaying in her school uniform, carrying her load of books. The man gave her the glass and she took it nervously, but she did not drink. She took the glass of water and satisfied the hunger from which she had been suffering.

The chicken and potato chips disappeared from their plates, and the man turned to his brandy. Nancy took two gulps of her strong drink and felt it burning down her throat. She bit her lower lip, looking down at the table. The man said to her with a short laugh,' You sure are a schoolgirl. That is the softest drink I've ever come across.'

'He is lying,' Nancy thought. She did not voice her accusation, but she took another gulp and poured more Coca-cola into the glass, diluting the whisky. The man emptied the brandy that remaining in the bottle into his glass and drained it with several huge gulps. Nancy peeped at his watch; it was already two o'clock.

'You won't take any more of this?' he asked, pointing to the bottle of whisky. A streak of heat moved from her head down, throughout her body. She shook her head at him, meaning that she would not take any more. The man corked the bottle, grinning.

'Finish and let's go,' he said. She nodded, took three successive gulps then, with a sigh, put the almost empty glass on the table. She refilled the glass with Coca-cola then drank again. The figures in the café blurred. Nancy winced, wiping her eyes quickly with her hand. The figures remained blurred. The man helped her up and they walked out.

You've made me drunk,' she accused him when they were in the car. He laughed childishly and leaned against her shoulder. She tried to move away but was too weak to move an inch. He touched her breast gently. She sonya'd, but could not put up any physical protest. He put his arm round her waist and pulled her closer to him; she leaned helplessly against his shoulder. He drove eastwards towards the beach.

* * *

At half past three she came fully to her senses. The man was rubbing his rough chin on her bare breasts. Her bra hung loose on her neck. She slid away and pushed him hard. He did not move. She sat up, staring at him with blazing fury. The man smiled. She sonya'd.

'Cool down, baby. Do you want to spit in my face after all the good I have done you? Did I do wrong when I picked you with my car, and offered you a drink which you accepted warmly? Did I?' The man spoke in a low voice, commanding yet pleading. Nancy cooled down. Her shyness returned and she dropped her hard stare.

'Take it easy, baby,' he said, placing his hand on her breasts. She removed it off, but her reactions were now less violent.

'You are an old man,' she said.

'That is beside the point. Being old does not signify sexual inability, and it does not show any lack of love or tenderness, it is completely beside the point in these things.' His voice shook until it choked in his throat.

'It is immoral, I am even feeling ashamed, sitting here with you and arguing with you about this,' she said. Her lips nervously chewed at the collar of her blouse. She yanked her bra down and fumbled behind her back to hook it.

The man continued, 'It s not immoral. Morals are creations and we make them in respect of the age in which we live. According to how we act, that's how we create the morals of our society. Our society in this age does not outlaw sexual relations between young and old.'

She looked at the buttons of her blouse as she fixed them slowly into their holes. The man put his hand into his shirt pocket and took out a hundred-shilling-note. One of her buttons was missing; he had torn it off during his survey- made without her consent- of her body.

'You should consider me as your daughter,' she said. She had not seen the money. She pulled the last button slowly, bit it between her teeth childishly, then fixed it.

'That is the most ancient way of defending your unfairness to me,' the man said, laughing lightly. He put his arm round her shoulder and pulled her closer to him, saying, 'Take this for a start.'

Nancy opened her mouth wide, staring coldly at the hundred-shilling note. The man smiled.

'No!' she said, 'I'm afraid to.'

'Hell. Why fear? This money is just a present for you. I am not buying you nor am I taking you as a prostitute. I respect you, so take it please and don't annoy me.'

She kept biting her blouse collar, a faint, scared smile on her lips. The man shoved the note into her hand and squeezed her fingers so that they might not let it go. He sighed heavily and sank into the driver's seat.

Nancy squeezed the note tightly in her fingers as she moved restlessly in her seat. She felt it tentatively with her fingers, then pushed it into her skirt pocket. The man embraced her and kissed her hungrily.

'I'll take you to my home for an hour and it will be over for today,' the man said, after doing a bout of self-service kissing and embracing.

Nancy said nothing. The man started the engine and they moved along Ocean Road, then Upanga Road into a small street called Mirambo. They came to a halt and the man jumped out to open the door for her. She hesitated, and he pulled her out almost forcibly, then walked her along a lane which led to a huge building with a name painted on its peak in big letters; J. MAGEGE 1963.

The man lived in a luxurious place. He lodged in the eastern wing of the three-storey building. He had divided the block into two parts, east and west. A European lived in the other portion. 'My wife has gone home for the rest of this month. So you can pop in here at any time!'

She kept biting her blouse collar and reading the ridges on her fingertips, numbed by the situation. 'What am I doing?' She did not realize how she came to that house. Time had drifted to five minutes past four! Being away from her home in the company of such an old man scared her. She was betraying Deo, she was betraying everybody, her mother would cry, Miss Barefoot would not like it… Why did she take the money? The thought of having accepted the money made her feel she was not very different from her mother. She hated it, she wished it would all come to an end. Fear and self-accusation dinned a loud 'NO' in her mind.

She wanted to shout it to the world, but her lips were dead; they shouted it to her own stomach instead. The man went into a room, leaving her in the sitting room.

'There are no people in this city,' Nancy thought. 'There are only strangers. What you do is only to yourself. That is why my mother is a whore. That is why this man could pick me up despite my young age. This is not a village. Why should I fear? Just a quick game and it will be over. A hundred shillings in my pocket.' She was confused. There were too many contradictions. She could not decide upon the right thing to do.

The man came out of the room. He took a key and locked the door. He turned to her and kissed her. She did not respond.

'Come this way, please,' he said, and led the girl through a corridor, up some steps to a second-floor room.

* * *

'Mami Nancy!' a voice called at the latrine door. Maria had just had a customer. She raised her head slightly to answer 'Oi!'

'Are you busy?' the voice asked from outside.

'No, go on in, Mami Joseph,' Maria answered, knowing who was calling. She spilled a few drops of water on the floor of the latrine and walked back to the house. Ana was still talking to another woman outside. Maria entered the house, picked up a towel and dried herself, then moved to the business bed. As she slowly straightened the bedding, Ana called again and was told to come in.

'Eh, you are very busy these days,' Ana said.

'Not in the daytime, most of them come during the evening.'

Ana took a stool from under the bed and sat on it. Maria sat on the bed, her legs spread. Her bored face made her look older than she was. Maria was middle-aged. Ana was a little older than Maria but her everlasting smile made them appear the same age. Ana was a mother of two: Joseph and a girl who was four years younger. Maria had conceived twice; the first pregnancy resulted in Nancy, and she aborted the second one. Ana came from Arusha, too. She and Maria had been together since they came to Dar es Salaam some twenty years back. Their first meeting was when Maria was employed as a barmaid in a bar called Gateways. Ana was then a veteran barmaid. They both came from Arusha, and somehow, from the beginning, that seemed to seal their fates together. Later, Ana was sacked from the bar and took refuge in the streets. After a few months Maria was also sacked. She joined her colleague in the streets, where they roamed waiting for men to pick them up for the night. They never had one lodging place; sometimes they had to sleep with the guards outside Indian shops when no one picked them up.

After a year in the streets Maria decided to be a 'home prostitute' waiting for customers to come to her own house. She moved to the Kariakoo area near Livingstone Street and settled there. Ana joined her after a short time and they had lived as neingbours ever since.

'Where is Nancy,?' Ana asked.

'I don't know why she is late. Their lessons end at three on Tuesdays.'

'You can never know with the children of today, she might have met a boy and they have gone for a walk in the streets. The world is that way,' Ana commented as one who was a veteran in those things.

'Ah say!'

'Yes, but it is their world. We can not lament.'

'But this is too much, with Nancy,' Maria complained.

'You will not believe me when I tell you that Nancy was brought in a Benz at six o'clock on Saturday last week.'

'Ek!'

'Yes, and she was in school uniform with her books. She didn't report home till then…'

'Heaven forbid!'

'And believe me, Ana, the man with her is the manager at Mountain Goat Rubber Factory. Do you know that man?'

'No. how did you know he was the one who brought her back? Did the girl tell you that?'

'No, she did not tell me, but I saw them when I was escorting that part-time husband of mine to the door. I know that manager, I have known him for a long time. To tell the truth, he once slept with me.'

'Jesus Christ!'

'I have not spoken to her about it. To make things worse, I have noted her twice, drunk.'

'Does she drink, too?'

'Like hell. The first day she was swaying like a palm leaf when she came home with a friend of hers. The other girl, too, was dead drunk, she could hardly walk home. A boy escorted her.'

They fell silent. A car honked outside. They stood up and peeped through the slightly open door. It was a Peugeot 404. A girl was running after it. She was not very young, but her age contrasted sharply with that of the man in the car. Ana sank back into her seat.

'Who was it?' Maria demanded. 'Another old bull after a teen-aged girl,' Ana said, pushing her stool nearer to the fire, which was almost dying down.

Maria sighed, her face contorted in despair. They call them "sugar daddies", she said.

After a pause Ana spoke up, 'I don't know why these young girls get attracted to such old, sexually weak fools... Those bosses use their height in this city to win the freshest and most beautiful young women. They ruin them...'

'Jesus, what a rotten lot! And we say we have leaders, we have an ideal government, while some fools dirty it for their bestial satisfaction.'

'You are right. Most of these sugar daddies are government officials, they use government cars and government allowances to win young girls. No "private businessman" would fool around with his hard earned money!'

'God forbid. It is hard to imagine a respectable, fat-bellied boss tumbling on a girl of fifteen!'

'Let me tell you, Ana, I know them. I know how they act,' Maria said, giggling and walking with her stomach pushed forward, 'let me show you.' She pretended to be driving a car. She stopped the imaginary car and came out scratching her head as if it were bald. She coughed slightly, blowing hre cheeks full and then releasing the air with a faint cough. Ana laughed. 'You want a lift in my "Pijot?"' Maria said, gesturing with an expansive, up-turned open palm to the imaginary car. Ana giggled.

'Karibu,' Maria said, and pretended to open the door for her friend. She started the engine and drove off.

'This is my apartment, not very big, it costs me just about a hundred thousand shillings.' When she spoke she stressed the words 'thousand shillings' and Ana laughed wildly. 'Come in,' Maria told the imaginary girl and kissed her. She pretended to close a door, then held the girl by the waist, leading her to the bed next to Ana. 'Now let me do it. Take this twenty-shilling note first.' Ana chuckled, then broke into loud laughter when Maria dramatized the bedroom activities of the old man. She acted out an orgasm which brought Ana's laughter to hysteria. Maria laughed, too, as she sat upright on the bed.

'I'll be damned if a manager could do that!' Ana said, still laughing.

'It is true Ana. You see a man dressed like a gentleman, talking with the most appreciable manners. This is the greatest hypocrisy in some of our "leaders". When you see such a man chasing after schoolgirls, you can never respect him...'

"These are the same hypocrites who say that prostitution has to be abolished! Who are the prostitutes, if not them! They already have money, they already have their wives. What have we?'

'Nothing. These same fools come to condemn the dumping of babies in latrine pits, the same ones who say that pregnant schoolgirls should be expelled from school, the same ones who plant the babies inside them...

'What do they think happens to the sperm they spray into the poor girl's wombs?'

'Hell. And they claim they went to school, where they studied the human anatomy!'

A long silence followed. A radio outside announced that it was a quarter to six. Ana looked at Maria, and the latter smiled back, shaking her slightly.

'But don't their wives satisfy them at home?' Ana asked, breaking their silence. Maria sighed and lay on her side.

'In that case, it is not very different from the question of our customers. Anyway, those sex maniacs want all the women on this earth! She said, closing her eyes.

'Hodi,' a voice called, and then the door was opened wide. Nancy stood for a few seconds at the doorway, then walked in, greeted them and went on towards the sofa-bed where she dumped her books. They said nothing to her. Ana told Maria that she was leaving and Maria went with her to the door. When they parted Ana said to her friend, 'But Maria don't stop her. After all, she gets lots of money from them. We are not very different from her.'

'What?' Maria exclaimed with her mouth opened wide. Ana added nothing more.

II

The sharp whining of mosquitoes stirred the room. Nancy moved restlessly on her sofa bed. Her mother slept soundly on the bed next to hers. A mosquito landed on Nancy's brow, and she slapped hard at it but the unharmed insect buzzed away triumphantly. She cursed. Again there was a buzz and the insect landed softly on her arm. She tapped lightly on the arm with her palm, and this time she got her target. She cursed the dead insect as she brushed it off.

'I wish I had money,' she whispered, pulling the blanket to cover her body up to the neck. People with money could do all they wanted with their surroundings, they could buy mosquito nets, air conditioners or fans for protection against the heat of Dar es Salaam, good houses, cars – everything. She wondered how Magege with his wife and two kids could occupy such a big portion of an expensive house. And it was his own! But how did he get all that money? She wondered whether all managers owned a Benz and a big, expensive house. Or was Magege very different from the rest of the managers? She lay quietly, reviewing the events of the past few days. The thought of the hundred shillings which Magege paid her for her 'company' made her sit up and shove her hand under the pillow. It was there! She pulled out the note and felt it with her fingers. She had decided to buy something expensive to wear. A beautiful blouse, some brightly coloured bell-bottom pants and that was that. She would be swinging like other girls on the streets, confident about her clothes. At first she was afraid that Deo might notice because she had no good clothes other than the ones he had bought for her. Now she would prove to him and to Rosa that she was not what they thought. She smiled to herself when she remembered how cheaply she had obtained the money. The fool had bought food and drink for her, had taken her to his expensive home. All the money he had spent on her, plus the money he gave her, unasked – all ended in the weak old man tumbling on her like a drunken dog.

Breathless after their bout, the old man had lain on the bed naked and tired. Nancy sat up and stared at the man beside her, at the hairy stomach, the fat belly, the smoothly shaven chin.

'Yes, Nancy said to herself, 'I have discovered the technique and I must use it.' She thought about how the man would drain his money into her. Yes, she was going to make him share his money with her by forcing outings upon him. She would pretend and he would fall for it, thinking she was in love with him.

'To hell with school! I'll go when I wish.'

She would surprise Miss Barefoot with the worst report ever. 'Only big men's children went on with schooling and had good job opportunities in the end. This is what everybody says in town. I am a prostitute's daughter.' At first she had thought school would redeem for her the privileges which other children got. Now she saw that had been sadly mistaken. Inclining her hopes on education would spoil her chances of obtaining money easily; she would be staying at home reading, instead of having the happiness other girls had.

There was Deo. She needed him and longed for his approval. But she feared that her teacher, her mother, her lessons, would only intrude on her important affairs. No, she was convinced that she would only make money using her body.

The mosquitoes stopped whining when several of them at last were able to land on her naked arm as she went to sleep, the money still in her hand. A dim lamp on the stool near her bed glowed softly on Nancy's innocent-looking face, the shadows of fear, ignorance and indecision receding in the weak light.

III

The bus stopped and Nancy stepped out. All the passengers looked at her as the bus moved away from the stop. She was on Upanga Road. She had to look for Mirambo Street. As she stood there, confused, a passing car honked. She turned round and looked at it. The driver was waving his hand as if asking something from her; he exposed his open palm to her, making the same gesture that street boys use to ask for sex from girls. She ignored him and proceeded along Upanga in search of the small street. Another passing car honked. This time it was a Benz, and the man inside looked like Magege. Yet the manner in which he waved his hand indicated that he did not know her. She waved back, however, and the car stopped. The driver reversed to reach her position. He was not Magege.

'Can I help, good lady? A lift?'

'Excuse me, I was just looking for a street called Mirambo along this Upanga Road.'

'Oh, come, I'll show you, get in.' The man opened the front door for her. She hesitated, but when the man looked at her with his mocking eyes, she got into the car. They had driven only a few hundred metres when she saw the sign: Mirambo Street. The man drove on.

'No! Drop me here. I'll not go beyond here!'

'Now, now. Don't be cheeky, girl. Take this if you don't trust me,' and he offered her a twenty-shilling note from his trouser pocket. The girl struck off his hand and the money dropped.

'I did not tell you that I was looking for money. Now please drop me off or I am calling the police straight-away.'

The man slammed on the brakes and the car came to a sudden, screeching halt. She opened the door and when she had put one leg out, the man pushed her out violently.

She cursed him back and walked along the way they had come, towards the street sign. They had actually only gone a little way from the spot where she had noted Mirambo Street.

Beads of sweat collected on her brow and started to stream down her face. She took out a handkerchief and wiped her face. She was walking fast and her bell-bottoms swayed to and fro in a fast, harmonic motion. She came to the sign that she sought, then walked along Mirambo Street, checking each building as she passed it.

Soon she saw the block-shaped building. It stood tall amongst a swarm of similar beautiful buildings, none of which were quite as tall. Colourful shrubs and flowers adorned the foreground like the edges of a tablecloth. The curtains were open and she knew he was there. Her heart beat with fear and anxiety. Again she wipe sweat off her forehead, making sure that her appearance was smart, then she pressed the doorbell. She could hear the buzz stirring the dead quietness of the room to life. A chair moved, and she herd it knock against a table. There were footsteps, then the door swung open. She smiled at him. The man did not smile back. He directed her to the sitting room, pointing the way with a wave of his hand and a jerk of his head towards the room. Nancy's face assumed the nervous, drawn image of a small child going to be spanked by its father. She walked in, accepting the offer. The man closed the door and followed her.

'Good afternoon, thank you,' Nancy answered, the words pronounced through her half-closed lips. Her eyes searched aimlessly on the carpet. The man stood up lazily and walked to a room. It was a kitchen. Bottles knocked each other as he opened the refrigerator. He came back into the sitting room with a glass and a bottle of wine. He put them on a stool next to her.

'Serve yourself, please. Meanwhile I have some work to finish. I'll be through in no time,' he told her. She chewed at the collar of her blouse shyly as he went to a table covered with a bush of files and papers.

When the man finished working with his files, he piled them into a heap weighted down by a heavy book. He stretched his body and the bones cracked like dry sticks.

Nancy looked at him and smiled stiffly. The man went to her. He sat on her side and started caressing her thighs with his fingers. The girl sighed. 'I'm going to play my part now,' she told herself. After taking a large gulp of wine, she rested the glass on the stool.

The man put his arm around her shoulder. His breath smelt of cigarettes. She tried to avoid it by resting her head on his chest. He passed his fingers savagely up and down her back, then bent low to kiss her on the lips. She giggled and lowered her head more to avoid his lips, then swept her palm softly up his back. His breath came fast and his heart throbbed violently under his shirt. He undid his shirt buttons, pulled off the shirt. He undid his shirt and threw it towards the table. 'Make money, girl,' Nancy told herself. The man was sweating. He walked to a fan nearby and switched it on.

'Are you ready?' he asked. The girl raised her shoulders, then lowered them fast, indicating that she was not ready. He made an attempt to caress her. She slid to the other end of the couch. He grunted.

'Will you be ready soon?' he asked nervously. She twisted both her lips to one side in a smirk, then relaxed her mouth. She meant 'no'. The man moved to her. She stood up and went to another couch. He hissed furiously. They looked at one another for some minutes. The girl was smiling and the man was furious. From her seat on the couch opposite him, she gently opened and closed her thighs without stopping. The man was stirred wild.

At last he drew a twenty-shilling note out of his pocket and offered it to her. She raised her shoulders and lowered them. Her eyes widened and rolled appealingly. He came to her seat, stretching out the hand with the twenty shillings to her. She shifted back to the first couch. The man's jaws were now tight with anger as he drew another twenty-shilling note and put it on top of the other. She smiled but did not move. Her thighs stopped swaying. The man walked to her. She let him sit close to her as she took the money, shoving it into her trouser pocket. The man lowered his head and she let him kiss her. After a spell of kissing and caressing, he took her arm and led her towards the bedroom.

* * *

The session was over. Nancy pulled on her trousers and dressed properly. The man lay back on the bed. She moved to him after she had dressed, and started pricking and fingering his sides. She grabbed him and rolled with him on the bed as she kissed him vigorously. Stimulated again, he stretched his arms to embrace her. With a giggle, she leaped to the door, opened it and said, 'I am going.'

He gasped helplessly on the bed. She stood majestically at the door with a broad smile.

'Give me a double sum and I will sleep here the whole night with you,' Nancy said. Her eyes blazed bewitchingly. She blinked them rapidly. The man jumped out of the bed and walked straight to a coat nearby, and fished out two twenty-shilling notes from it. He showed them to her. She laughed and said, 'I told you a double sum. If you haven't got that, please let me go.' Her voice had changed into a business-like one. All the innocence had vanished, all the shyness and fear had been absorbed by the sharpness of the words which she uttered.

'Please…' the man pleaded. His voice was hoarse and the words stuck between his lips. She felt sorry for him. She walked to him and, taking the money, she kissed him softly on his lips. She put the money in its place, then encircled him with her arms. They fell onto the bed and lay there for the night.

'You are the winner, girl,' Nancy told herself.

Part Two

Sugarcane' Interwoven

DEO

I

The mellow, full voice of Isaac Hayes filled the room. 'I don't know what to do with myself,' it crooned, and the harmony of the saxophones, drums and guitars behind the voice turned the room into an auditorium. Deo lay flat on his bed and let the music swallow him. He was holding a paperback novel in his hands, but he was not reading it. He wanted to read but when his eyes rested on the letters, thousands of images came into his mind. He did not want her to keep haunting his thoughts, he wanted to banish her from his brain and wait for the day to come when church bells would ring in their ears. He feared thinking about Nancy because it always led him to wild imaginings about what kind of wife she would turn out to be. Her family background was a huge, dark cloud over the splendour of her beauty.

Since the day he had asked her to marry him, an endless fear kept running through him. He had committed himself. What would his relatives say when they heard that he was married to a prostitute's daughter? 'Mtoto' wa Malaya!' they would say in Kiswahili. They would despise him. His friend, Frank, had thought quietly for a moment when he told him about it. In the end, Frank said the decision was 'alright,' but he appeared unhappy about it.

His brothers would not accept it. His father would just laugh, and then perhaps look at him with derision. Then his mother, what would he tell her? Obviously she would hate the idea. She had suggested to him earlier that he should get married to Joyce, a clergyman's daughter who was schooling at Ashira. He had refused. The girl was not the type he wanted – a gloomy, unpenetrable type of girl whose deep religious faith made boys dread and ignore her presence.

He loved Nancy. She was open and sensible – maybe. He did not know beyond that. The girl was totally unaware of the family into which she would come. Yet she appeared ready to accept the new life with a sincere openness. She believed in and respected him, she almost feared him, and he enjoyed it. He knew he could weave her into his own pattern. That she came from a prostitute mattered very little, sometimes, when he reviewed her qualities in beauty and behaviour. She was still pliable, he would change the prostitute's blood, make her into a beautiful, loyal wife. What did the comments of the others mean? He did not give a damn about any of them. It was he who was seeking a wife.

The music stopped and the room became gloomy. Deo jumped out of bed and went to put more records on the automatic record player. Someone rapped on the door.

'Karibu,' he said and started the music. Frank walked in, grinning broadly. Deo shut the door that opened to the bedroom and came back, taking a seat opposite Frank.

'You were sleeping at this hour, in this frying Dar es Salaam heat?' Frank said, looking at an old Sunday News.

'Not really sleeping. I was kind of... meditating.'

'Ah, yes, I know. You were up to it again. That girl gives you nerves.'

'Ah, no!' They laughed at this. Deo took his novel from the bed and dug into it. They were silent.

'You know, Frank,' Deo broke the silence before he had hardly read a page. 'I have gone to her mother and confirmed it.'

Frank blushed at this. He stared deeply at Deo and the latter simply smiled, triumph gleaming in his eyes.

'Yes, I went and had a good talk with her. You can just imagine it.'

Frank looked at him and shook his head in despair. 'Tell me how it was,' he enquired at last, and Deo recounted the whole story to his friend. He withheld the bad scenes: how he had arrived and met a man coming out of the house buttoning his trousers, how he had called at the door after waiting a few minutes outside. He had walked in only after she welcomed him from inside. When he went in, the woman stared at him blankly. He knew she was expecting something other than what he had gone for. He was nervous. She did not recognize him.

'What is it, boy?' she said the words said with a vulgar, business-like intonation. He had to speak quickly or the drama would flare up into a whirlwind of confusion.

'I am Deo, Mama,' he said and the woman, as if struck by a thunderstorm, sank down on a seat. She offered him a stool and he sat on it, his eyes searching the dirty earthen floor. A rat ran across the room. Deo moved his legs quickly, drawing them into a crouched position. She made attempts to speak but seemed to have nothing to say to him.

'I have come here, Mama, to tell you that I am engaged to your daughter. I want us to get married after she leaves school.' He said it, releasing her from her suffocating tension. She did not say anything at first. Her eyes glared into the wall and her half-smiling face relaxed slowly into an expression of exultation.

'I have heard you, son,' she said at last. Her vibrating voice stung deep in his heart. He dreaded the word 'son' coming out of her mouth, directed at him. She smiled broadly and her brown coloured teeth gnawed at his nerves. Suddenly he became aware of the smell in the room. The woman sat relaxed on the bed, almost unconcerned. He imagined her in many positions, deftly plying her trade. The memory of that man he had passed on the little path to the door, who had obviously been a customer, made him quiver. He had to leave quickly he felt himself positioned in front of a lioness' jaws, facing with guilt; her presence stirred him into deep rage and self-accusation. Why take a daughter from such a woman? His eyes drifted to the disorderly bed, to the flies searching tirelessly on it. The flies never despaired, they were present on the bed, in the cupboard, on the plates… everywhere. He looked towards the corner, at the pail of water with a piece of soap stuck on it, and cringed inwardly.

'I am going,' he said and the woman smiled, thanking him for his visit to confirm their new relationship. She wanted to escort him to the door. He refused.

Thus Deo narrated the event, withholding the most unpleasant aspects. He told Frank that the woman was different from what he had expected, that she was good-natured, only that she sought money through her body that she could not do otherwise in jobless Dar es Salaam.

'Man, you really have guts, being engaged to that girl,' Frank said.

Deo gave a slight laugh. 'But what is the difference between her and other girls?' he asked.

'Nothing different physically, or anything material in her present appearance. But my friend, Deo, I am telling you, we grow up with our natures and we act according to what nature has taught us…'

'Yes.' But if your words mean that because the girl sprang from a prostitute's house, that nature taught and brought her up in prostitution and that she would, as a result, end up as another prostitute after our marriage, then I strongly disagree.'

'I don't want to build a mountain out of an anthill,' Frank said, 'but I am only trying to give genuine and open advice. It would help if you thought it over yourself.'

They dropped the topic and both began to read. The music stopped and Frank put the same stack of records on to play again.

II

On Monday Deo felt bored with his work in the laboratory. He laid down the apparatus with which he was working and went to the mixing mill. There he was welcomed by a huge clamour. Everyone was taking in the loudest voice he could manage. Deo avoided the thick of the mob and went to sit on a tank not far away. Hands shot into the air, swayed and shot downwards. Other men, instead of merely gesticulating, rapped empty tins to emphasise their points. Some who had nothing to say, but were hostile to anything that was condemned by the crowd, applauded those who were speaking, danced or made ear-splitting yells.

'No pay, no work!' one yelled and another joined him, with 'No work, no us.' Then a third one added, 'and no us, no production!'

Then another one… Deo traced the stream of phases through the clamour till he made a full stanza out of them:

No pay, no work!
No work, no us!
No production, no factory!

Then no manager, no threats of being fired, no fatigue after being overworked, etc, etc. A young, muscular man in overalls joined Deo and sat on the tank just next to him. the clamour was growing bigger. Other workers in the compounding section and from other nearby sections walked onto the scene and fed the crowd of workers with new phrase-makers, new yellers and new clappers. Those from the compounding section had very raw tongues.

'What are they complaining about?' Deo asked the young man who had come to sit near him. The man sonya'd and shrugged his shoulders. He shook his head thoughtfully, then his desperate eyes turned to Deo.

'It is this managing son-of-a-bitch,' the man said, his lips quivering, 'I'll skin him alive if he delays our money further than now. I'll rip into his g- -d- -Benz and wipe off that sugar-daddying smile of his. I'll…' The man fired his words into Deo's ears, saliva jetting through his teeth not regularly. Deo felt uneasy. The man was angry, and Deo was trying to avoid the explosive words but the man was cursing so loudly that the others looked at them, laughing. Deo moved to another tank without the man even noticing it.

'What is it all about?' Deo attempted another enquiry after staying cool for some minutes. He was speaking to an elderly man who appeared more calm that the first one.

'Ah, brother, you know these problems of wages. He who has eaten enough does not realize that there are others who are still hungry. Take an example-myself. I have six children, four schooling. All of them expecting the three hundred shillings I earn to make them live. Thank God we survive through these inhuman conditions. At the end of the month we have no extra coin with us. Now imagine when the wages are delayed for three days, and this is the fourth day. How are we going to survive?'

'Is it the first time to have such delays?' Deo asked, trying to appear as concerned as the man himself.

The man smiled disdainfully. 'First time? Hmmnn, you big boys sure don't worry about us. You work there at your desks or whatever the-hell. You get your big pay early, you are happy with the money, and forget the real industry of this factory, the doomed men. You forget that we have never had early wages since this factory started to be managed by that son-of-a-whore. You sure have no worries about us!' He, too, became angry.

Deo was dismayed. He could not explain to the old man that he was not the one who arranged the payment of workers' wages, that he was as much concerned as they were about the issue of wages, though his salary was always given to him on time. They sensed that he was a man different from their class. He hated that he was unable to help them and make them believe he was sympathetic to them.

Deo was grateful when a foreman stepped over to relieve him from the old man, who was still yel ling at him. 'Now Mzee Mashaka, this is not the manager, let him go,' the foreman said to the excited worker. 'And you, friend, you'd better go, this is not your place, they'll eat you alive if you stay.'

Deo felt humiliated as he walked towards the lab. A group of workers turned to him and sonya'd, then resumed their shouts.

Deo went straight to the laboratory and slumped himself into a chair. He picked up the office telephone and buzzed a messenger to bring coffee. Nobody replied. He put down the receiver.

'What's wrong, my friend?' asked an aged Indian man with a fat stomach, which he pushed before him as he crossed the threshold of the door. He was puffing huge clouds of smoke and the choking fumes of tobacco that made Deo cough. The Indian smoked the Crescent and Star brand.

'Mzee Ramji,' coughed Deo, with all that money you receive monthly, you are still smoking that noxious brand of cigarettes. I'd swear you are extra stingy.'

'Don't talk that way, friend,' Ramji said. 'If you knew how many of our businesses are in financial problems, you wouldn't say so.' A worker passing outside peeped through the window and sonya'd loudly. The Indian blushed. The worker had gone. Ramji turned to Deo, looked at him for a few seconds then turned away. 'Damn Africans,' he said.

'What?' Deo snapped and eyed the Indian severely.

'No, I was only saying…eem…that…

'No, you. If you don't watch that tongue of yours, next time you'll be in trouble, I tell you, you will meet real trouble. Don't forget where you are. Either you decide you are with us, a part of us-not better or worse-or…

The Indian was the production manager of the factory. He was employed as a clerk a few years after the establishment of the factory. Later he was promoted to production officer and an African who was holding that post was demoted to foreman. The African threatened to resign and the general manager, Magege, agreed to make him an assistant production officer. The African was the only man with a diploma in rubber technology.

Deo marched out of the laboratory and to the staffroom. There he was told that the manager had gone to seek help from the police. The telephone exchange was locked and a group of angry workers were guarding it.

Suddenly a van stopped outside and a couple of newsmen walked through the gate. They went over to the knot of workers nearby. The voices of the workers were quiet and the rapping of tins had stopped. Deo went straight away to join the group as the newsmen interviewed the workers.

'I am ready to stop working if this rat does not change his behaviour. Last month he delayed our wages, this month he does the same, next month the same. Bloody swine. What shall I eat? What does he think my children live on? Sand? Brother, do they eat sand? Or does he expect me to go into the streets - begging? I have nothing to sell in brothels!'

'Excuse me,' a reporter intervened, are you alleging that your major problem here is this delaying of your monthly wages?'

'No! so many problems, brother, so many. This is only the most urgent. If you want me to tell you all that makes this factory stinking, I am afraid you will be sick. So much has to be done, and

I fear only a little will be done.' The old man was cooling down as the words came out from his incensed lips. He was Mzee Mashaka.

'What other complaints do you have apart from this issue of the delay of your wages?' the reporter asked.

'You are supposed to know, I mean I expected you to know a lot. I hope you do know a lot,' Mzee Mashaka said, with a mocking smile. His teeth were charcoal black. The cluster of workers close around him stirred into a collective chuckle.

'Look here, young man, you are a reporter, aren't you? Yes, you are. You are a learned fellow, aren't you? Yes, you are. You don't know problems – a worker, you don't know me. Now stop this demagogic politics, stop this nose-poking of yours into our world. We are fed up. I am not a kid, everyday complaining and none of my complaints are heard. A man comes here breathing between buttocks and stomach, fat and softer than gruel. He speaks through his nose, "I want to know your problems here," or "We are not racists, power to the workers and peasants…" and more and more nonsense. What is this politics? There is a working person at Mountain Goat. There is a big man with his political blah-blah living in Oyster Bay, where all the big men live. The big man speaks about the working people at Mountain Goat but he doesn't know really what the man at Mountain Goat is. I am fed up!'

Mzee Mashaka became disturbed again. The other workers asked him to cool down, and dragged him away. The reporter went on and faced other workers. One said, 'Our other problems, my friend, are the oppression exercised on us by the employer. We are being exploited. The owners of this factory are West German capitalists.

'They are from Frankfurt and they come from there every six months or so to collect their luck. What pains us so is that their interest is only in the money, not in the makers of the money. To them we are nothing.'

Another worker said, "We have no freedom of speech. Each worker is alone with his muscles and that's that. I don't know what Juma thinks, I don't know how to complain when the employer threatens to fire me. We have no organized body that backs us workers, that unites us, nothing…'

An old worker, wearing dusty and ragged clothes that, even among that group, stood out, said, 'Look at me. I am supposed to be the one who produces those huge heaps, those tons and tons of sandals which lorries come every morning to collect and take to I-don't-know-where. Am I...' this system of the goddamn, mangy capitalist bootlicker, Magege, carrying out decisions and orders without summoning the workers. He goes and gets orders from the "foreign consultants" of the factory... he shoots them to us without asking for our recommendations.'

'Can you express yourself better, please,' the reporter said.

'Express myself?' The youth was sarcastically incredulous, but he immediately took hold of himself and continued. 'Yes. Look here. Let's say I am manager. I come and say "today we shall stop work at noon." Why? Because I have an appointment with my sugar baby, or because the cream of the cream of the factory employees are having a party, or because Ramji is having his daughter married, and so forth, now, I come tomorrow and say, 'O.K., today we shall compensate yesterday's work since we had a half-day off, we shall make seventy-five sheets of rubber instead of fifty.' What is this? I'll be damned if they know how tired a man is after this toilsome job. How can one do a two-day job, just because Magege had his 'business' with his young girls? I am young, I also need outings. But I can not go out because I get home too tired, too exhausted to go anywhere...'

'Why don't you let him go for his outings and remain at work the full day so that you don't have double work the next day?' the reporter asked.

'Man, when the big people are out, you also have to be out. They don't trust us, you know. They'll always say to you, "Fix those rubber strips." They don't know how to fix them, but they'll never trust you to fix them on your own!'

The reporter laughed. The workers sonya'd at him. Deo grunted his exasperation and Mzee Mashaka, who had returned to the scene, rolled his eyes upwards.

'Have you any more allegations against your manager?' the reporter asked them.

'He's a puppet!' one said.

'The sugar daddy,' a woman spoke up. 'Fires a girl a few days after he has hired her and played about with her!'

'The money-swindler!' another called out. And one shouted, 'The tool of the exploiters to oppress us!'

'The poisonous...'

Thus the workers rained raw words on the ears of the reporter, who was rapidly backing away towards the van to avoid the gesticulating hands.

Suddenly, there was a siren and the crowd dispersed shouting, 'Police! Police!' Deo fled into the laboratory, his head ringing with conflicting thoughts.

III

In the afternoon Deo walked with another man to the bus stop. They were co-workers in the same laboratory. They talked a little about the morning's events, then Juma, the man, asked Deo: 'You are not afraid, sharing a girl with your manager?'

'What do you mean?' Deo asked tonelessly.

'I mean, aren't you jeopardizing your post?' Juma asked again.

Deo was startled by his emphasis on the subject.'

'Am I sharing a girl with my manager? He asked. He wrinkled his face slightly to show more respect for Juma's question.

'Well, I was just asking and trying to caution you that, as well as I know Magege, this relationship with the same girl will put your job in danger.'

'But, Juma, don't make me shiver when there is no cold. Have you seen me going out with any of Magege's girls? Such old and bumpy women!'

'Now, Deo, let's not make a court case out of this. I will tell you one thing, and you just try to calm down till I finish. Last year we had a young man called Eliud. He was a senior foreman. I don't know how he shot so fast to that position! This man started a relationship with a certain girl who was one of Magege's part-time girlfriends. I admit that the girl was extremely pretty and young.

Eliud did not know at first, that he had befriended the wrong type, the kind who, in these times, is really only for the big men. We discovered the thing after seeing him take the girl out several times. We warned him. He ignored our warnings. A few months later we heard that the boy had been sacked. I don't know whether he got any job after that.'

'I am sorry,' Deo interrupted, 'I get your point, but please, I don't see where or how I come into it. Tell me who this girl is, first.'

'Ah, yes. So you are not aware of it. Listen. I know that girl of yours who stays on Livingstone Street. She is a schoolgirl, I suppose, though I am not very sure. She is yours as far as I have seen your movements together. But sincerely, Deo. I warn you that I have seen Magege with her on several occasions, most of the time when she was being driven home by him. I have a brother who stays on Livingstone Street and I pay frequent visits to him. You and Magege are, so to speak, being interchanged by her...'

'Are you telling the truth?' Deo asked, amazed.

'Truth. Allah curse me for lies,' Juma swore.

A bus hooted in front of them. It was going to Kinondoni. They both embarked, occupying different seats. The bus moved off and Deo paid double fare to the bus conductor.

Double dealer, Nancy? No, it is not possible! He could not believe it. Nancy was too young and innocent to play such a dirty trick on him. He must have forced her, the swine, taking advantage of a young girl's naivete. He would get back at Magege, he must pay for this. Deo was sick; a cold rage wove his thoughts into a complicated pattern. He wanted to yell or go cursing into his office. Anger choked painfully in his throat. He cursed silently and it made him more agitated.

The bus sped along Kilwa Road, fast and quiet. It was surprisingly empty. During those hours buses were supposed to be full, people being sqeezed by the hundreds into a single bus. But this one was empty; the conductor must have skipped some bus stops to avoid overworking himself.

Workers. The work flashed through his mind. The conflict that morning had aroused in him the glimmerings of understanding.

What were the workers, really? He began to realize why they acted as they did, why they were frustrated, why they had malice towards anyone who identified himself with the 'big people' in their society. They were desperate, they viewed their future and the future of their children with resentful pessimism. The workers were not so much concerned about 'respect' and 'moral values', because their own human value was subordinated.

They spoke freely, cursing as much as their rich street vocabularies allowed. They eased their frustrations by socializing; sometimes they drowned them with alcohol. The men patronized brothels. Of an evening they roamed the streets apathetically. When at last their apathy was replaced by hostility towards the existing order of things, they flared up and fought it.

At Mountain Goat Rubber Factory, they tried to fight against the positions in which they were placed. They failed. The forces that were always used to assure that the status quo was maintained, the police, were called in to kill the vigour of their thirst for change. Now apathy would resume and no change had been achieved.

Deo asked himself whether he didn't have a responsibility, some task before him in the workers' struggle. He had an urge to act, to fight, to overpower-what, he didn't know. He had to find out, he had to go deeper into this thing. Suppose there was no private owner of the factory, suppose there was Magege, suppose the workers whose sweat produced those heaps of rubber sandals-suppose they each had a contribution to make towards the factory's progress, and each possessed an equal right, share and responsibility to the achievements of the factory...

The bus stopped and Deo stepped out. As he walked home, the brisk rhythm of his steps rhymed with his thoughts. 'I will fight Magege, and all those like him, because of Nancy, because of Mzee Mashaka.'

* * *

He did not stay at home when he arrived. He had to see the girl. After having his lunch and clearing away his small domestic matters, he went straight to Nancy's home.

Her mother was there. There were no customers. He went in, greeted Maria and begged her to let Nancy accompany him on a short walk. She gave her permission and the pair walked out across the tarmac road, then along Kondoa Street. The street was sandy and their legs were drawn back each time they made a step forward.

'Do you know the law that governs the difficulty in walking on the sand?' Deo asked, smiling.

'No,' Nancy answered. She was struggling to move across the sandy area to a hard soil path nearby.

'Newton said, for every action there is an equal and opposite reaction.'

'How does it apply in this?'

'You see, when you take a step forward and force yourself ahead, you lean on the leg that stays behind and the force that you apply forward is equally applied backward; hence the sand, being loose, lets you push it back and you move half the distance.'

'Heh! You know so much physics!' Nancy said, extending her right palm to him.

'It is not only physics, it is life,' Deo rejoined, and his palm met hers in a sharp clap. They laughed.

'And life…?' Nancy asked childishly.

'Yes, life. It is never straightforward. You have to struggle and there will always be forces trying to keep you back. You have to fight and conquer them. Whenever you try to push forward, there will be forces of retrogression and you have to overcome them in order to succeed. In a society or any group of people or a country like ours, we may try to make a long step forward but, like walking on this sand, there are equal backward and forward forces. Only when progressive forces surpass the retrogression of reactionary forces do we have progress. Otherwise reactionary elements will always keep us behind or sometimes push us even further back.'

'Heh! Deo!' exclaimed Nancy as she closed the gap between them.

'Newton was unknowingly very profound in this statement, although perhaps he did not intend to be so profound. For example, now: I love you. I have decided to get married to you. There will always be temptations to break our ties. Sometimes such forces are created by the lovers themselves or sometimes by social elements against them. One has to conquer these to prove the steadfast love he has for has beloved… such things are very difficult to do in practice. Often, we fall victim to temptations.'

'I say!' Nancy cried out, then, grabbing his swinging arm, she squeezed it and said, 'Deo, you are overloading me, next time I will come with a notebook.' The pair laughed cheerfully.

He took her to Uhuru Gardens. They sat under three coconut palms which formed a triangle enclosing them with broad leaves.

'Nancy,' Deo began after a long silence. His tone was more serious. 'I have a few questions to ask you.' She looked at him, her face innocently unaware.

'What are they?' she asked, a slight quiver in her voice.

'Do you know or have you ever seen a man called Magege?'

She was quiet for some seconds, as if trying to gather the names and faces of all the people she had ever come across. Her face showed that she was slightly shaken. She answered, 'No, I don't remember having heard such a name. Why do you ask? Have you had some problems?'

He searched her face, and tiny wrinkles appeared around his eyes and mouth. He doubted her answer. She blinked her eyes rapidly. He stared deep into her, then he said, 'Do you know any man? I mean have you known any man other than me?'

"No,' she said nervously.

'Have you ever been driven around by a man in his car? An aged man? A big money man? A fat-bellied, high ranking officer in a Benz…'

'No!' she cried. 'No man has ever gone around with me other than you! Unless you have some other intention, please, you'd better change the topic.'

'Don't get angry, I am only asking.'

'Yes, I am going to flare up if you press me with these unfounded, accusing questions. You know I have never gone with any other man and you…'

'Aaah, let's drop it!'

'O.K., let's drop it, but next time when you want to get on my nerves, please warn me as early as possible.'

'But I was only asking,' Deo pleaded.

'You ask when you are thinking something or when you imagine that something is wrong somewhere. And such questions are always accusing.'

'Was I accusing you?'

'You were not, but your questions were.'

'Are questions accusations?'

'Sometimes they are. This time they were.'

'Let's drop it.'

'O.K.,' she agreed, but she was still frowning.

IV

'Sugar daddies,' said Frank, 'are a few irresponsible government bureaucrats, who are with no good political justification, privileged to occupy high posts and obtain large sums of money. They make money through big salaries and underground businesses or through naked corruption. They make more money than they need, and use the extra to seduce women and destroy young girls, schoolgirls. They forget their high ranking position in the government and become moral dirt, betraying the society which put them into leadership. These are sugar daddies.'

He took a gulp of beer. He and Deo were drinking in a small bar. The bar was half full but the noise of drunk people, and the music from a jukebox switched on to full blast, made the place sound crowded. Two barmaids were dancing around a certain crazy, drunken man. He swayed before the jukebox. The barmaids danced, following his movements, and they kissed and sang into his ears. He had a Tusker beer bottle in one hand; his other hand played about with the coins in his trouser pocket.

'You see him?' Deo whispered, pointing to the drunk. 'He has been buying beer for those barmaids since we came here, probably earlier than that. They are now all drunk and people say that man takes no less than two women to his whenever who knows where. He gives them lots of money, too. Is he a sugar daddy?'

'No,' said Frank, 'but he is as much a prostitute as those two barmaids. I know him, he is a big man in the Kibo Match Factory. Sugar daddies don't take women who have been used by hundreds of men. They take fresh crop, they drink at the source of the stream and sniff roses which have just bloomed. A sugar daddy ambushes a schoolgirl or a new girl in an office, or a girl who is looking for a job. He goes to bed with her and she gets the job. He seduces a schoolgirl and buys her a wrist watch, he sleeps with an office secretary and gives her a promotion.'

One of the barmaids came and sat next to Deo. She giggled, and then offered an empty glass for him to fill it with beer. He did so. She pulled her chair closer so that her body touched his. He sighed, and she smiled at him and then put her arm on his shoulder. Despite Deo's annoyed frown, she continued to grin drunkenly.

'What is it?' he asked her.

'Nothing,' she said. 'How do you feel about it?'

'What?'

'Are you cold? Aren't you taking me tonight?'

'Have I ever taken you?'

'No. but I was just asking. Heh! Some men are hot-tempered! Are you cold? Or has your man gone into the sea?' She put her hand on his shoulder. Deo took it off.

'Go now, and come later. I might change my mind,' Deo told her and returned to his beer. Frank laughed at him, his face remain down-cast and his shoulders jerking with mirth. Deo sonya'd. The barmaid moved to another table and joined a group of drunks who were shouting and singing. She put her head on the shoulder of the drunkest of them and kissed him on the cheek. The man grabbed her hips with one arm and touched her breasts with the other. She squealed with pleasure.

'I hate it when these barmaids take it for granted that I am here for anything other than to be served my beer,' Deo said to Frank.

'They are trying to make a living. You give her a pound, you stay with her the whole night.'

'So that's the horrible way of living we are arguing about!'

'No, don't get me wrong. It is not horrible as such. To them it is business. The towns are somehow so much more attractive than the villages, even if there is no employment for the women who come, except for the sugar daddies who employ them, seduce them and fire them, then their only refuge is prostitution. From the point of view of some people it is a kind of relief. Some see it as filthy and some take it like a bush at the cross-roads – it serves like a latrine but needs to be cleared.'

'In other words, prostitution serves several purposes,' Deo commented.

'Yes. Even the trade of bhang brings wealth to those who grow it.' The barmaid was coming to them. Deo winced. A man called her, and she attended him going for the beer he ordered. When Deo saw her turn away to the bar, he grabbed Frank who broke into loud laughter.

'Well, as far as you have described the sugar daddy, I do support you,' Deo said, trying to draw attention away from himself, 'but my point was that prostitution should be eradicated. It is true that prostitutes at Kisutu and elsewhere, who are old in the profession, are different. First, they cannot live otherwise in this Dar es Salaam. Second, it is the only refuge for unmarried workers and jobless town boys when they have a sexual urge. And some people take the position that, if there were no prostitution, the courts would be full and flooded with rape and other immoral sex - related cases.

'But it can be eradicated,' Deo continued. 'I am sure that it is possible to wipe it out, though it would be a hard task. I've been doing some reading. Did you know there are no prostitutes in China? Do you remember that after the fall of the U.S.- backed government in Vietnam, the revolutionary government ordered all prostitutes to be rounded up and sent to new areas for a productive existence?'

'But we need a complete change in our attitude towards life for that to be able to happen here,' Frank said. 'Men and women would have to be re-educated. Prostitution can be done anywhere, even in the rural areas. The town folk could go there and follow the prostitutes!'

'True,' Deo agreed. 'It is not possible to cure the malady under present circumstances. Too many of our political directives are hypocrites; some people say the main principle seems to be: Let... the politician not shut his mouth.!

'So we come to a compromise,' said Frank, 'because, as you said, as long as our society is full of vagabonds, low-paid workers, and so many jobless roaming the streets, killing prostitution will remain a dream. The whole issue comes down to money, a capitalist attitude. People need money because, in a town, it is the only means of getting what they need to live. It appears to them as the only thing that closes the gap between them and the class of the big people, wabenzi. They become thieves, killers, whores, and what not. To get money. All of the people that we say are spoiled, they are all like victims of a war; they are the fruits of exploitation. Thugs, dope pushers, pick-pockets, pimps…they are all our making, we let them be. Without many other things in our society changing from the roots, ending our hypocrisy and selfishness, our cry against whores will remain a madman's cry.'

They fell silent for some time to nurse their words; then in compromise Frank extended his palm to Deo, who smacked it loudly. They laughed.

> Jasho la ngamia, anakula Mwarabu
> Ulimwengu wa samaki
> Mkubwa kula mdogo.
> Yarabi napofuka
> Giza limenizidi!

The song was taarab. Trombones, accordions and flutes hailed the words with prolific richness. Deo smiled at the sense of the poetry; it illuminated his recent experience at the factory. The song roughly meant.

> The Arab eats the sweat of the camel.
> In the world of fish,
> The bigger ones feast on the smaller.
> My Lord, I am see nothing,
> Darkness has blinded me.

He and Frank were now in a hotel called Rainbow, a good distance from the first small bar where they had been drinking. Rainbow was a peaceful place where one would always meet Swahili women dressed in dark robes, accompanied by their men, dressed in the manner of their culture, and confident. The heads of the men were covered with very clean, white caps tattooed with patterns of black and red thread. The taarab band played at one end of the bar in the hotel, and a group of Swahilis would always be sitting calmly, listening to the music, taking soft drinks. With the singer, they would move their heads in approval or disapproval of the meaning of the poetry being sung.

At the other end of the bar where Deo and Frank were sitting, other customers – more caught up in the new 'town style' of life, as if in isolation– drank hard liquor and joked. They rarely listened to the taarab.

'I like that woman,' Frank said and they both laughed.

'What's good in the woman?' Deo asked.

'Beauty,' Frank answered and Deo chuckled.

'What is good in the song?' Frank asked.

'Truth,' Deo answered and Frank frowned, pondering his friend's meaning. Deo smiled and said, 'At the factory this morning…' he narrated the whole story about the strike, '…and the manager, like an Arab ordering his servant to flog the camel when it refused to walk, ordered the police to attack the workers with clubs,' Deo concluded.

'But what has that got to do with the song?' Frank queried.

'After the strike, I though about the fate of the workers versus that of dishonest leaders. It is not any different from this song. I mean the fat word-feeders, they are not any different from the Arab or the big fish in the song.'

'You might be right; poetry is very flexible.'

Frank's 'beautiful' woman, the Swahili woman, walked out towards the toilets. Frank grabbed his bottle and dashed to a seat in the corner where he was sure the woman would pass him upon her return. When she re-entered the bar, Frank approached politely and coaxed her to share his company. She agreed after a long exchange of words.

They came to sit at the table with Deo. Frank ordered a round of beer for all of them.

'Who is he?' the woman asked Frank. She had one gold tooth, and her wrists were covered with golden bracelets. She was of middle age and average size, with full breasts and big hips.

'My brother, my young brother,' Frank said, nodding to Deo. The latter gave a mocking smile. Again Frank nodded towards the woman, still looking at Deo.

'My latest best friend,' Frank said and the woman smiled. Deo struggled to hold back an explosion of laughter.

At midnight the taarab band stopped playing. People were emptying their last bottles of beer and Deo, sitting at the table near the door, was quite bored as he waited for Frank and the woman. She was struggling to empty her remain beer bottle in huge gulps. Frank was close at her side, his arm locked round her hips.

The bar closed and the trio left in a taxi which dropped Deo first at his apartment.

LABYRINTHS

I

A car honked outside. Maria raised her head and peeped through the small window, expecting to see it, but it was not within her view. She lowered her head and sat sluggishly on a stool charcoal glowed brightly in the earthen cooker which heated the small room into a semi-oven. She wiped some sweat off her brow and picked up a knife lying on the edge of the cooker. Before her was a small heap of cooking bananas. She began to peel one as she hummed a taarab song. The car honked again. This time the honk lasted longer. She cursed. 'Why doesn't he get out of the damn car and go himself to the one he is calling?' she wondered. She envied the one who was being called upon by a car-owning customer. Some of them were lucky. They had customers who gave them large sums of money, paid their rent, and sometimes took them for rides in their cars. Such prostitutes were usually still youthful, not very different on the surface from other girls in the streets or elsewhere in town. Some were even luckier; they were able to coax the car owners into being part-time husbands. Maria had never been lucky, apart from the rare days when a drunk customer would come a dump all his money for a single 'hit'. One day, a drunken young man had come into the house without knocking or saying 'hodi' at the door. She yelled and cursed at him first, attempting to scare him away. The man did not move. He thrust his hand into his dirty trouser pocket and collected all the money inside. He gave the whole amount to her. Maria took it and put it in her purse, then drew out a long, bright knife, placing it near the pillow, ready to defend herself if the fool tried to claim back his money. She gave him the usual service. She was astounded when the man simply waked out peacefully when they were finished.

'Hodi!' somebody called at the door. Maria put the knife on the heap of bananas and walked to her bed.

'Come in,' she answered.

A man opened the door and stood at the entrance motionless.

'Magege!' she exclaimed to herself. A streak of anger, fear and hatred shot through her veins, her skin brightened in the fire's glow as she broke into a sweat. Magege took a few steps towards her.

'What do you want here?' she asked him coldly.

'Excuse me, mama,' Magege said humbly, smiling.

'I was only trying to see whether Nancy was around.'

'What do you want her for?' she asked abruptly.

Magege was a bit shaken. He gathered a few wrinkles on his brow. He was obviously fumbling for a sensible lie. Maria drew back, moving restlessly on the bed.

'You see, the young lady came to my office a few days ago, looking for a job. I promised her that I would try to find a vacancy for her and fix her into it!'

'But she is still schooling', Maria emphasized.

'I know. But she said earlier that she was completing her studies at the end of this year.'

'And you have a vacancy for her as early as now?'

'Yes. You know, when somebody has such a deep interest in your factory, you try to consider his or her application.'

They paused for a long time, as if studying each other and preparing words for another session of the hot dialogue. The man stood there, breathing between his fat belly and his fat buttocks. Sweat streamed down his face past the clean-shaven chin, dripping onto the hairy patch of chest that showed through his shirt collar. Maria smiled at him, her face curved into cold, infuriated sarcasm. She sat carelessly on the bed, and her wide-open eyes searched the man with a scarecrow's rage.

'I will not say anything to you, Magege,' Maria said,'but I want to warn you about one thing. Stop this cat-and-dog chase with my daughter. I know the lies of big men when they want to hook their fish. I am sure it is not the vacancy which brought you here. You are a sugar daddy and I will not allow you to get a bite of my daughter. What? You are cursing…'

'Cursing? Cursing, eh…' Magege said as he moved to her, his first clenched.

'You'd better stay away from me,' she said, pulling the long knife from under her pillow. She wiped it with her palm and waited. He stopped a few metres from her. The woman stood up.

'Get out!' she stammered. Her voice exploded out of her breast and fired into the streets. The man backed towards the door, his eyes all the while fixed on the knife. She shouted at him, called him all sorts of horrible names, spat at him and followed him to the door with the knife pointed at his stomach.

'Make whore! Shameless bastard!' she shouted at the door as he sped to his car. Outside people had gathered to see what was happening. They joined Maria and booed at the manager as he ran. A stone hit the rear window of the car and others followed as he accelerated down the street. The people yelled at him, calling him by his name. They knew him.

II

That evening Magege went to Kilimanjaro Hotel for a drink. The incident at Livingstone Street had drawn a black mask in his mind. The memory of that woman sneering at him and spouting dirty words, the mob of thugs and whores booing at him and kids fearlessly stoning his Benz enraged him. He feared and dreaded the dirty eyes which photographed him and painted the image of his clean face onto their filthy minds.

His drink was served to him and he swallowed the first gulps almost without tasting. He felt a strong, drowsy wave sweeping slowly through his veins. It was whisky. When he had soaked himself enough to feel boozy, he started moving his eyes aimlessly around the room, looking with keenness at the faces which came into his sight. Suddenly at one corner of the room he noted a pair of youths, a boy and girl, both of whom came into focus with a familiar brightness. The young man: tall, slim, smart, his hair combed into a round bush. Deo. And the girl: beautiful and young, dressed in her favourite bell-bottoms and a white blouse which framed her smooth face in the dim electric light. It was Nancy.

He cursed himself. The whisky burned down his throat as he drained half his glass. He coughed. Again he looked at Deo, and the figure of the youth wove in and out of the labyrinth in Magege's mind. Deo was a bush thicket which grew between Magege and his aims. He was striking worker, cursing Magege and smearing his position with obscenity, telling news reporters what kind of man Magege was. He was a street thug, a veteran of Livingstone Street and his dirty mouth jetted filthy words, booed and yelled at Magege. Hell!

Magege emptied the last of the whisky bottle into his glass and drained it with successive gulps. He ordered rice and chicken, ate it all, then picked up his car keys from the table and walked out. At the door, he took a glimpse at the couple, sonya'd and walked away.

III

It was a bright, cheerful Wednesday morning. The clear sky and absence of sea breeze forecast a hot day. Noises in the streets resumed, and the blare of a few radios added to the roar of people, the rumble of lorries, buses and factories. Nancy snored in her mother's bed, the one that was not used for business. Maria had a customer that whole night and she was exhausted. The man was still asleep though was late in the morning. She had to prepare for the day-time customers. Flies blanketed her bed with a living cover. The night had been hot and active. She had given an appointment to the wrong man. Usually she passed nights with men who were not very energetic.

Hodi!' somebody called, and swung the door open.

'Nancy, we are late for school!'

'Who is that?' Nancy mumbled, half awake.

'Rosa. I said, we are late, why aren't you awake? Are you not going to school today?' Rosa asked.

'No, I am sick. I have a headache.'

'Ah. I am sorry. Then be calm, just sleep, it must cool down soon,' Rosa said. She stayed at the door for some seconds, then said, 'Nancy, I am going,' and closed the door quietly. Nancy could hear footsteps as Rosa strode to school. Her head ached. She lowered it painfully onto the pillow and tried to get more sleep. Sunshine brightened the room as it poured through the uncovered window.

Maria woke up, stretched herself and searched the room with wide-open eyes, as if looking for something lost. There, Nancy slept, snoring like an elephant sleeping fearlessly in a game reserve. Maria sighed with pain and concern. Such a short while ago, she would have charged and spanked the girl on her behind. But Maria could not go against the girl's wishes, for Nancy would flare up like a wounded buffalo.

As a mother, Maria was impotent, just watching her daughter being carried along by the strong current of evil. Sometimes Maria wanted to grab Nancy and beat her, or yell and curse at her, or call death to come and wipe Nancy out of her vision. She didn't, and the girl stubbornly let the strong current carry her towards doom. 'It is bad to bear a woman, it is a curse,' Maria would say. The memories of the girl's childhood made her wish she had aborted the pregnancy. To her, the world was always bitter.

Nancy had changed drastically during those few weeks after the first meeting with Magege. Her mother had noted it, but there was something which stopped her form taking any action; there was a fear that she would trigger something into explosion.

The engagement with Deo was confirmed; the boy had come to see Maria a few days back and stated his honorable intentions. Now Nancy was sidetracking, moving out of the clear path into complexity of movements which Maria saw as wrong. There were the days she had come home drunk, escorted by the old man. There were the days she had slept at some man's place that Maria did not know in particular. Yet Maria did not say anything; she just observed and quietly protested the whole thing. At first Maria had thought Nancy would take her words seriously when she warned her about Magege. She did not want to report the same thing over and over; those words were heavy on her lips. It was as if she was making a confession to her daughter.

Now Nancy had proven stubborn. She had felt the touch of city life and accepted its false warmth before Maria could block her way. Nancy was convinced that what she was doing was right, and it became more and more difficult to convince her otherwise. If Maria used force and became very strict, the girl would move further away from her. And the boy would drop the engagement. The world would never give her a chance to win! It was always there to claim her joy. It made her a prostitute, and she served prostitution faithfully. It went on and made her break a taboo; she slept with her brother and conceived a female child. Now it was claiming back the child and pushing her to prostitution even after she had put all hopes on her.

She walked to Nancy and shook her softly. The girl woke up and looked at her mother with a weary, angry face.

'Why haven't you gone to school?' Maria asked.

'I am sick, mama. I have a headache.'

'Say you have a hangover, not a headache.'

'Not a hangover, Mama. I am sick,' Nancy complained.

Maria spat on the floor and walked out to the latrine. The girl rolled on the bed, cursing silently. Maria washed her face with cold water and rinsed the rest of her body quickly. She emptied the pail of water into the latrine pit and walked back to the house. A few flies trailed desultorily behind her; others surveyed the shut door of the latrine.

'If you go on becoming cross with me this way, we shall soon part. You will have to look for your own home and your own mother,' she told Nancy, 'you will have to face your world on your own.'

The girl shrugged, pulled the curtain to one side and walked weakly through the entrance. She walked a few steps then turned back to face her mother.

'Mama, if it seems to you that I am being cross, when I am actually sick, then I also see that I'd better look for a new mama.'

'And I don't want to talk to you in that hangover of yours. Wait till you are sober. I don't talk with drunken children,'

'I tell you I am not drunk!' Nancy sputtered as she swayed towards the latrine. Maria sonya'd vehemently. She washed a teapot with a small amount of water and poured the contents on the dusty floor. She took a few handful of charcoal and put them into the cooker, then sprinkled it with kerosene and struck a match. She threw the match into the charcoal and it lit into a huge, smoky flame.

When the tea was ready, Maria called her daughter and they took their breakfast quietly. Neither commented on the quarrel which had been going on. They munched the bread and washed it down with gulps of tea. At times, one would glance at the other, then quickly withdraw her gaze. After finishing all her bread, Maria swallowed the last of her tea and put the cup on the floor. She went back to her bed.

'I will warn you about one thing, Nancy,' Maria said.

'You said you will not talk to me till I am sober, Mama,' the girl said. Her eyes were cold, her grin expressed mockery and stubbornness.

'This you must know whether you are drunk or drinking or praying in the church. Listen!'

The girl turned sharply to her mother with eyes inquisitive and childishly bright. Maria looked at Nancy's face, at her expression, which showed total unawareness of the dark sea in which she was swimming. Maria felt pity.

'I don't want you to become a whore. You will one day see how important my words are. I have experienced this thing and have felt its pain. If you dog-track old men like Magege for their money, they will spoil you. With that money they give you, you shall not buy anything that will help you recover from that destruction. It seems a lot of money but it is a lot of evil. This is the second time I am warning you on the same subject. Now you have gone further, you are making yourself an all-time woman for all types of men. I am that kind of a woman. Have I achieved anything in my life? Ana and many others, have they made it up to the top? I love you, my baby, and you are the only person who will shed tears at my grave. Nancy, don't make me weep for you as if you are dead before I have died. I have always wept and my eyes are drained. You can only make me laugh. You have never tried, you have always demanded tears, you are now demanding blood from them, my eyes…'

'Mama!' the girl gasped, tears starting down her cheeks. Maria talked on, her accusing eyes blazing with a painful emotion, her lips twisting with the vigour of torment.

'Nancy,' she said at last, 'you are engaged to Deo. The golden chance, this one. Think of the consequences after you have spoiled your engagement.'

* * *

That same morning, Magege was in his office at the factory. He sat behind his desk doing nothing. A messenger brought a newspaper and put it before him. Magege was motionless, his thoughts shifting from the event at Livingstone Street to the factory workers' strike. He lifted the telephone and dialed.

'Manager here. I told you I want Deo Mataka to report here. This is the third time I am dialing you.'

'He is coming, he was just preparing some…'

'Tell him to come here and stop telling me what he is doing,' Magege shouted and put th receiver down. He picked up his newspaper and started passing through the headlines. On page three there was an article by the Roving Reporter which read: Why Misunderstanding At Mountain Goat Rubber?

He sighed after reading the first paragraph. The article seemed to be totally against him. the first few paragraphs talked about maladministration and misunderstanding between the manager and the workers. There were two paragraphs which described him as an irresponsible manager who was always after female secretaries and young girls. That shook him. One read, 'The workers told me that the manager, Mr. Magege, is always going out for private business or looking for girls, young girls…'

As he read, the story absorbed him; Magege felt a wild contempt for the author of the article and the workers who had spoken with him. Someone knocked at the door and swung it open. Deo walked in and Magege indicated a seat to him.

'You are Deo Mataka?' Magege asked.

'Yes, sir,' Deo answered. Magege stayed quiet for some time, digging deeply into his own mind to find a suitable beginning. Deo glanced surreptitiously at the newspaper open on Magege's desk and read the headline from the Roving Reporter article. He shrank back into the chair nervously.

'I called you here, young man, in order to settle the silent war between us.'

'What war, sir?'

'Wait and listen. I know you know about it and I will not let you play a childish trick on me.'

'But, sir, I don't understand. If it was the strike, I...'

'Shut up and listen. I don't want a quarrel with a man of your age on this issue. I also don't like the way you are behaving to me as your manager. I want this thing to stop. If I see you with that girl again, we'll see who is more potent. I want to talk it over with you in a friendly manner, but I can see you are taking me as a blind fool and as your equal. I am cautioning you...'

'But Mr. Magege, which girl are you talking about?'

'Shut up! If you are engaged to Nancy, I am going to shatter that engagement of yours. I preceded you in this affair with the girl. I do precede you in everything. You can go on loving her if you want, but you will weep for this eventually. I am giving you my first warning.'

Deo leaned on the chair, his mouth wide open and his eyes staring at Magege in disbelief. A teardrop rolled down his cheek. He did not wipe it off. Five minutes passed, but Deo kept looking at Magege with a helpless, angry face. 'Juma was right!' Deo kept repeating silently to himself.

'Get out and go to work! You are consuming business hours with your private matters. Go on. Get out!' the manager barked, and Deo walked out of the office, wiping his face quickly with a handkerchief. His steps towards the laboratory were like those of a wounded sheep.

Magege fumbled for the newspaper and looked into it without absorbing a single word from it. He felt a bit relieved; he could at least look after some of his affairs. The emotional speech he had made to the boy had eased his tension. The boy was vulnerable and he, Magege, was the obvious prize-winner.

'Now, how to deal with that whore?' he thought. Could he sweep the dirt between him and Maria away? There was no dirt, she was herself the dirt. Now, how to tackle her? Employ a gang of thugs to raid her, rape her and butcher her. At least she had to pay for the humiliation she had splashed in his face. How?

'Trrrriiiiiingg!' the telephone buzzed. He lifted the receiver, it was from Leopard Plastics Industry Ltd; they were lacking some chemicals and they wanted him to help them with some from Mountain Goat, if he had a big stock in 'his' stores.

'No problem, Mr. Mhina, you can come and we can arrange it,' Magege spoke into the phone, and the other manager agreed.

'Don't forget our plans for Monday, friend,' Magege said.

'I will castrate myself if I do,' his cohort replied, and they put down their telephone receivers simultaneously.

Immediately Magege picked up the receiver again and dialed a number. He fumbled aimlessly with the pages of the newspaper as he waited for a reply.

'Hello, Labour Relations Office.'

'Hello, will you put me through to Mr. Mgoda,' Magege told the operator. Silence. Then 'Hello, Mgoda here.'

'Good morning, Mgoda, this is Magege.'

'I say, ndugu! How was it yesterday? You did not let the eggs slip off your palms, I hope.'

'Not really. Anyway I told that boy at the Customs to take the rubber from the Customs store to home. You know what is to follow.'

'Damn, I'm not talking about that. I know all about that, and since it is a simple matter, there's no point in talking about it. I was asking about the spring chicken.'

'Hell. What a topic for the telephone! You must trust your telephone operator too much.'

'My God! You are not the Magege I used to know. Who's taken your guts?'

'The paper.'

Oh, the paper!' Mgoda exclaimed and broke into a chuckle.

'I am serious. You haven't read all of it, I'm sure.'

'Such a dispute is too simple; we needn't even talk about it.'

'Mr. Mgoda, you must be mad. That thing about the complaints of the workers is serious. If Mzee gets the full information about it, he is going to explode. You know, the politics in the allegations are very touchy, and the assassination of my character…'

'Ah,' snapped Mgoda, 'the character assassination, yes. It might be a bit disappointing as far as you are concerned. But the workers' grumbles are nothing to worry you. I am here. I will make everything alright. The select committee which will come to study the situation there will be under my control. The full report will have to pass through me before being handed over to Parliament for scrutiny. What's the problem?

'I hope you would say so. Now, at least I am happy. You know such things are not good for Parliament.'

'Forget about it. Just nurse your 'assassinated' character. You can buzz Ndugu Barabarani and tell him to teach his reporter what to report and what not to report. You know, I am fed up with this loudmouth "Roving Reporter" business.'

'You're damn right,' Magege said.

'Haya. Magege, make sure that the chicken is eaten to the bones.'

'Not at all; it's not help, it is responsibility. You know our status quo has to be maintained.'

Both men laughed and banged their receivers down.

IV

Deo had acted harshly that afternoon. He was relieved he had been able to do it, but it pained him that he had no other alternative. To tell her the right thing, which he did, was an admittance of his weakness. Like a man, he should have looked for better solutions. So, Magege was more potent than him! He was able to displace him from Nancy by simple threats-dangerous threats, as far as his job position was concerned. He had no alternative. Why should things be made in one way only? Why should fate bottleneck its chances in that harsh manner? His relationship with the girl was dead, then. He killed it. The relationship was a failure, and that meant also that something was lacking in his manhood; it meant Magege was more of a man than him. why?

At first, after the quarrel with Magege, the brightness in Deo's mind that was Nancy had become dull, and her richness withered like beans in the sun. Her image started to become faint in his memory. It danced tremulously as a passerby. Her presence was no longer needed; it was like a flower in the plains whose beauty was only visible at first glance. But those were only first, temporary sensations; now he felt different; he could see how much he needed her company. Yet he could not withdraw his decision, it would prove weakness again. He had to force himself to get her out of his mind.

Deo sat on a stool and observed the gloom coming to engulf him in his room. Everything seemed to have come to a standstill. His earlier optimism now stared coldly at him, then dissolved to nothingness. A long blackness stretched before him like a highway to death.

He put the light on. Its faint glow seemed to end just a few inches from the bulb. He looked at the tablecloth which Nancy had bought for him. Its colour, at first a bright pink had now been bleached to a dull grey. He looked away. In his pocket were receipts they had when they went to Kilimanjaro Hotel a few days ago. He took them out, tore them and dropped the pieces on the straw mat. When he tilted his head slightly, he caught sight of the wall where a picture of Nancy smiled, without partisanship, at him, and the Makonde carving hung nearby. Nancy's eyes were cheerful and her teeth bright. Her image glowed with beauty; the soft glow grew into a flame which caught him. His rage and hatred for Magege was like dynamite lying in his breast. 'He killed me, I shall kill him.' That was his thought, and the image of Nancy danced with it. He could hear her talking, and her lilting, playful voice danced lightly in his brain, endlessly.

That afternoon he had gone to the girl's home after work. The quarrel with his manager was still fresh in his mind. He had arrived at Nancy's house with his anger boiling like a pot of unpeeled yams. The girl had not gone to school. He told her that he had some words to say to her. She was shaken because the emotion with which he spoke betrayed the wrath he had wanted to hide from her. She accompanied him to a big mango tree just a few metres from Uhuru Gardens. He explained the whole incident with Magege, then asked her why she did not tell him before had that she was a two-timer. He cursed her and told her that if Magege fired him he would strangle her. She was a whore, he told her. The girl wept at this. At last, he told her that their engagement was no more and that she should never again visit him. Deo had left her crying at the mango tree.

He sat in his room, morose. He was gripped deep in his vulnerable heart by feelings of guilt and self-accusation. His restless hands picked up a book from the shelf. It was written by Christopher Okigbo. He opened it carelessly and found the last stanza of Heavensgate. It read:

Rain and sun in single combat;
on one leg standing
in silence at the passage,
the young bird at the passage

He hurled the book onto a table and leaned forward, his palms resting on his thighs.

'What is this?' he said loudly, and the bird from the poem danced in the rainy sunshine. Deo's tears showered the wings of the bird but the scorching heat of the sun dried the tears as fast as they landed.

'Magege and Deo in single combat, sun and rain in single combat!' The line of the poem drummed in his head impatiently.

'Yes, perhaps I was not very serious. Maybe I did not shed enough tears to soak the bird and bar it from flight.' He had dried his tears, and she could fly. High into the clouds… towards the sun.

Drowsiness kissed his eyes into sleep, but the words still drummed in his head.

* * *

A bad night. Nancy tried to sleep but the turmoil in her head wiped away all the sleepiness that she had begun to feel. Mosquitoes whined over her head and stung when she exposed any part of her body. She covered herself completely to avoid them, which made her feel she was in a grave. Sweat dripped from her body dampening the light khanga with which she had covered the sofa-bed. She could not uncover herself to cool off as the mosquitoes were there, waiting to sting.

She rolled about on the sofa sonya'ing and cursing. Maria snored. The noise reminded the girl that her mother was there. That reminder itself stirred Nancy into a guiltiness that exceeded even her frustration and confusion. Images of men haunted her vision. They were like morning shadow, tall, slim and ghostly. She looked at her mother as if expecting help, assurance. But Maria snored on, and the snoring sound came out like that of a barking dog scaring away thieves. Nancy found no company in the sound. The images remained intact.

Magege was a looming shadow that first came, then disappeared when she tried to focus on it more sharply. His chuckle reached her ears like a dusty wind; it grated irritatingly on her nerves. Magege was a vulture that came and went with a goat or a lamb. The vulture strangely did not fall victim to arrows or stones. Magege was a drunken wild dog. The dog sobered up only when he wanted to jump to another palm tree for more wine.

Miss Barefoot: she kept staring into exercise books and unfinished homework papers. The teacher's gaze penetrated Nancy's head and read all the dirty things she had done. The days she had dodged school, all her quarrels with her mother and all the money she had acquired dishonourably, all seemed to be within the teacher's X-ray power. The glasses on Miss Barefoot's face glittered with a desperate brightness.

Deo: he smiled, he grinned or shook his head with disbelief. His eyes were endlessly deep, crinkled at the corners; his ears appeared a bit higher than usual, like those of a scared goat. She and Deo shared a common youthfulness, they appreciated the same things, thought alike. Yet when she tried to join his world he jumped away violently, he sneered at her, he cursed her and suddenly he knew her as a prostitute. Her world remained isolated; there was a demarcation between the two. Let the other stay as far away as it wished. Her world was contented with itself.

And the image of her mother: Maria was weeping grievously. Nancy did not like the motherly way with which the image stared at her. She dreaded the clear reflection of herself in the sorrowful image of her mother. She did not want her mother or anybody else to grieve for her. But there stood her mother, weeping inconsolably.

Nancy looked at mother sleeping and suddenly their differences dwindled like a bush fire that was approaching green grass. Maria slept on peacefully.

Now Nancy's own image appeared. Perplexed, she was like a fowl that had lost its balance. She was drowning in an open sea, trying to grab something but only squeezing the water off her palms. Then, like a shark in the sea, Magege bumped her body with powerful fins, while Deo sailed away in a fishing boat, unconcerned. Desperate, sharks, she felt herself floating away, feeling more friendly to them.

She was sweating terribly. She threw off the blanket and swept her palm through the thin air. For some time the mosquitoes disappeared. Nancy fell asleep.

Part Three

Fire

FLAMES

I

Nancy was pregnant. She had gone to a private doctor at Umoja wa Wanawake Street after having suffered from nausea on several occasions and feeling a bit unusual. The doctor had said she was about two months pregnant. She told him that she was in school and that she would be having her examinations in November.

'Will it be known by the teachers before I do my examinations?' she asked the doctor. He frowned a little, thinking.

'I am afraid, yes,' he said. 'This is the end of June, you will have about five months before you do your examinations to the last paper, and you are about two months pregnant. They will know it.'

Then Nancy, amid tears, asked the doctor for any kind of help. The doctor told her that an abortion could be conducted but he was not in a position to do it. The case was dangerous and he complained that the police were alert, that his dispensary was under special observation. He suggested to her that some other doctors would be able to help her though they would demand a high fee.

That was on Thursday. She stayed two days without consulting any doctor. She had no money. She had used the hundred and fifty shillings she got from Magege last weekend to buy herself a pair of platform shoes. She feared telling her mother about her pregnancy; it would only bring tears and swearing. Deo was through with her. Her pregnancy would be a torturing humiliation if he were to know. Beyond these three, she had no one who would be able to offer her a large sum of money for such a purpose.

Now it was Sunday. She had made up her mind. She must see Magege about it. He would be able to help, he had money. Would he deny that he was responsible? Would he say that he did not know her? She had proof. She had a picture of him with her at the beach. They had taken it one Saturday when he took her out quite a few days after Deo had left her. He had two copies made and the girl had one of them. Her mother knew Magege, Rosa knew him and Deo. He would not escape.

She went to a telephone box and dialed his number. A young boy answered and she asked him to switch to 'Mr. Magege.'

'Hello, Nancy,' Magege said.

'Hello, darling. How are you, how are things?' Nancy answered. Her voice shook. She trembled as she held the receiver.

'Wonderful. But I am missing you.'

'Me, too,' she said; a short pause followed.

'What's up?' Magege asked.

'Em…em…can I meet you at four this afternoon?' she asked.

'Hmmn…O.K. But as you know my wife is around so we will not be able to stay out for a long time. Anyway, I'll make arrangements to meet you at exactly four.'

'Is she at home now?' the girl asked.

'Well, no. She has gone to church, but I am expecting her soon.'

'Ah. Then I had better hang up.'

'O.K. Let's make it at Princess Bar then.'

'Alright. I will be seeing you then,' she said and put down the receiver. She walked out of the telephone box weakly. A chilly sensation streaked down her body and she shivered. '…you will remember my words…I have experienced these things.' The memory of her mother's words pounded in her head like women pounding cassava meal. As she crossed the street a wave of contempt for Magege rose within her. 'Let him just help me get rid of it. I will never dream of doing those things again,' she thought.

Outside her house, she peeped and listened through the small window, then stayed outside waiting. Her mother had a customer.

II

Thin clouds had covered the bright, hot sun and cast a shadow over the city. She went to Princess Bar at a quarter to four. The place was not very far from her home. It was a combination bar, café and dance hall, all of which bore the name: Princess Bar.

She went into the café and ordered a cold drink. The place was almost empty. Two gentlemen sat near the entrance talking in low tones. A second pair, a boy and a young girl in her early teens, sat at the other end, opposite to her. The last man, an old man, fat and with a look of official 'responsibility', sat only a few metres from her.

Magege arrived five minutes late. She stood up.

'Nancy!' he exclaimed, paying little attention to the other people in the café. She went to him and shook his hand, smiling bashfully. The people in the café stared at them. Magege went to a man who was responsible for letting rooms. He asked for a key and paid for two hours boarding. They went to room number five.

'No cash today,' Magege said, when they had seated themselves on the bed.

'I didn't come here for that,' Nancy replied.

'What, then?' he asked, smiling broadly, almost grinning.

His hands started to explore the upper part of her body. She was cold.

'What's wrong? You are almost dead.' He stopped caressing her and eyed her attentively, his face frowning. The girl sat wordlessly on the bed, her body motionless except for the heaving up and down of her chest. He kissed her on the lips; she let him, but did not respond. He shrank back, disappointed.

'Eh! What's wrong, Nancy? You must have some thing wrong with you. Tell me.'

'I have your baby. I am pregnant,' she stated simply. Magege stared at her with his mouth open. His hands lowered onto his thighs, his body turned cold. A long silence followed. She waited anxiously for the next comment from him. The man looked at her shaking his head, then dropping his eyes, he sighed.

'I understand,' he said at last, 'I know what you are expecting now, that I'd put you off. No, I will not deny the responsibility I have in this pregnancy. I know I did it, and you have a lot of evidence, I know. I will not take you either, as a wife or something. You are not my first girl, and from those I have dealt with before, I know only one way out, if you will bear it. You will, I hope.'

'What is it?' she asked.

'You are a schoolgirl, you will not be able to go on with your lessons if you have conceived. I will help you to get rid of it. There is a doctor, a friend of mine.'

'Is it painful?' she asked, and her face revealed at last that she had been hoping he would suggest an abortion. Magege could not prevent his expression of surprise…

'Not very painful. It only needs courage,' he said. Nancy smiled. They kissed again, but now it was Magege who was no longer responsive. He fixed his shirt. The girl stood up and they marched out of the room at the café, the old man was still there, and the two gentlemen were still conversing. They all stared at the couple as Magege walked out with Nacny, his arm round her waist.

III

On Sunday evening Magege went to his friend, the doctor. Doctor Allan was a retired doctor from the government hospital in the city. He had worked as a private practitioner immediately after his retirement, about five years, and he was still single. Girls in the town called him 'Ndugu wa Tumbo.'[2]

'So this is the girl,' the doctor asked Magege, pointing to the picture that was taken at the beach.

'Yes,' Magege answered. He was reading a newspaper. On a small table before him was a glass of wine. He sipped some of it and sank back onto the sofa. There was no sign of disturbance in his eyes, he appeared totally unconcerned. The matter was a common one in his adventurous life. The doctor, however, showed a professional concern in the matter.

---

2. Brother from the same womb.

'But, John, this girl seems to be too young to hold it,' the doctor said. Magege looked up and smiled. He put the paper on his thighs and took a gulp of wine.

'Now, Allan, don't tell me that of all the cases you have dealt with, this one is the youngest. Don't be that cautious. You know, these days a girl can do many things which would have been impossible a generation past.'

'No, John. I am not being too cautious. The question of age is very important in this matter. I am not going to perform an abortion on a fifteen-year old girl.'

'No, Allan,' Magege said, 'I told you this girl is twenty years old. She has just been undernourished; that is why she appears young. I know her enough to judge her age.'

The doctor stared at the photograph again. He smiled at it. Magege laughed at him, the way he held the photograph, with care and deep concentration.

'You are nervous these days, Allan,' Magege said, laughing.

'No, John. I'll take the case, I am just appreciating the dish. You know, I have once come across this girl or one who looked exactly like her. She is really lovely!'

'Ai, ai! Allan, don't tell me you have once harvested a crop that I sowed.'

'Sure. I gave her a lift one day in my Benz. She slipped away, though.'

'That's better, it would have been war, you know. Sometime after this case is over, I'll drop the dish. Then it will be empty,' Magege said with a hint of pride.

'You will have to carry contraceptives with you next time. This matter sometimes becomes serious, and you are so keen in your long-range woman hunt!' the doctor said. Magege chuckled.

On Monday, at ten in the morning, Nancy walked through the school gate and went to a telephone box.

She dialed Magege at his office. When the operator had relayed her call to the manager, she said, 'Hello, this is Nancy. Have you fixed it?' Magege told her to hang on. Through the receiver, she heard the sound of a door being banged.

'Hello, I went to close the door. Now, I have already arranged it with the friend of mine, and we shall do it at his private hospital. Do you know a place near Uhuru Gardens called Kwacha Engineers?'

'No,' she said.

'O.K., then I'll pick you up at two in the afternoon tomorrow.'

'Alright, I will skip my classes.'

'O.K., Don't come late,' he said as he rang off. Nancy lowered the receiver weakly and put it back in position. She sighed and walked out of the box. At the gate she saw Miss Barefoot walking towards her classroom. Nancy walked rapidly to close the distance between them. They did not say anything to each other as they walked into the class together.

IV

The bus dropped her at Uhuru Gardens. There were no people at the bus stop. She hated people looking at her when she was wearing her school uniform. Many would know that she had skipped classes. She was afraid she might meet a school teacher in town who would easily note her. She crossed the street and joined the lane which led straight into the garden center. There was a bar there. She went straight to the bar and chose a chair outside. The bar was not operating at those hours.

At school, she had skipped biology class, and told Rosa to take care of her books. When Rosa asked her where she was going she had said she had an appointment with 'the old man' for a snack. Rosa told her to 'be careful.' Nancy had laughed bitterly at the remark.

She sat outside the bar looking at everyone who crossed her line of vision. Buses roared downtown, uptown, east and west. Small cars slid smoothly, carrying well-fed, well-dressed and well-brought up people. Huge lorries rumbled up and down the roads carrying stones, concrete blocks, iron bars and many small articles. Labourers piled on top of the loads and sang or yelled queer words to the people on the streets as their lorries passed by.

At last she saw the small, fat shape of Magege walking along the lane towards her. A streak of a cold fear shot through her body. She stood up and forced herself to walk down the steps. A few steps later, she joined him on the lane. There was a broad smile on his face.

'Hello Nancy!' he said, opening his arms and enclosing her in them. Her body shook nervously.

'Now, stop kidding around,' she murmured, forcing a smile onto her cold face. He laughed childishly. The girl blushed.

'It is two now. Let's go,' Nancy said, taking him by the wrist. He pulled her close and kissed her.

'Magege! You know I am in school uniform. Don't make everybody know this please.' He sighed and followed her. His breath smelt of alcohol. They walked to the Benz.

'I'll have to drive fast. Allan must be waiting now. It is a quarter past two.'

She was quiet. People on entirely purposeless walks swept past them with careless abandon.

'When the doctor asks you your age, tell him you are twenty,' Magege told her on the way.

'Why? But I am seventeen! She exclaimed.

'If you tell him your exact age, he will not be able or willing to help you.'

'So it is that dangerous,' she said after some time.

'Not at all,' Magege assured her, 'you know how cautious doctors are.'

The Benz sped down Uhuru Street. At a roundabout it swerved and swept along Independence Avenue. There was a tall building which sat beside a small iron-roofed building. He parked the car outside the tall building and they walked a few steps to the door of the smaller structure. A young man greeted them at the door; he gave Nancy a look of recognition. Nancy returned the same keen look and smiled. He was Joseph, the son of Ana. The young man did not smile; he shook his head slightly to show disapproval. Nancy hastened past him to enter the main room.

'Hey, John! Who taught you to keep time?' the doctor said with a grin.

'I am sorry. You know, at the office there were some visitors…'

'No problem,' the doctor interrupted, 'it's never too late. Take a seat, young lady,' he told Nancy.

This man! He was the same man Nancy had met when she was looking for the street that led to Magege's block. The way he talked, the way he was absorbed in staring at her, the fat, short body – he was the man!

'Come this way, John,' the doctor said to Magege. He looked at the girl and gave her a sarcastic smile. Shaken, Nancy sat restlessly on the chair, gripped by a horrible agitation. Magege followed the doctor into an inner chamber.

'Joseph!' the doctor called.

'Naam!' Joseph spoke with a hoarse voice that came out as if from the inside of a bottle. He walked into the inner chamber, passing Nancy who was seated in the consultation room.

He gave her a quick look and she covered her face with her palms. He did not stay long inside. When he came out he walked straight to Nancy and whispered into her ear, 'What you are doing is the worst thing you could do.' Then he walked to the door, closing it firmly. He laid a strong bar across it. The room fell into total darkness. She gasped with fear. He put the lights on and his accusing eyes met hers. She trembled slightly.

Magege poked his head through the inner chamber door and signaled with his hand for her to enter. She stood up, looked at Joseph, who had turned away, and then at the barred door. Hesitatingly, she walked to the chamber. Magege opened the door for her and then closed it behind her.

There was a bed, long but not broad. It had belts on all sides and was covered with white bedsheets. The windows were closed and two huge, black curtains covered them, blocking all light from outside. A lamp sat on the table which stood next to a big cupboard. Below the table was a red container which looked like a large bowl. In the bowl were small pieces of white cloth, perhaps they were tampons. On the table was also a large stop-clock which was not moving, some files and many papers.

The doctor asked her to sit on a chair. He opened the cupboard and took a syringe with two bottles. He put them on the table and took out a red plastic sheet, spreading it out to cover the middle portion of the bed. Then he put the large bowl near the bed and asked Nancy to undress.

She stood up, but did not undress. Her eyes surveyed the two faces in the unwelcome atmosphere of the room. She was confused. Fear and anger blocked her throat. She wanted to scream, but her lips could not open. Her legs started shaking violently. Magege looked at her, his face expressionless. She read in his very lack of expression, a horrid and murderous character. The doctor looked at her with the gentle, fatherly face often used by his profession. It was a humble look, and it contrasted strongly with the nightmare in which she was drifting. He took two tablets from a box and filled a glass with water.

'Take these pills, then,' he said to Nancy. She took them and swallowed them with water. The doctor asked her to sit on the bed. She hesitated, and her nervous hands took the collar of her blouse; she bit at the edge of the collar. A few minutes later, she felt her legs loosening and becoming limp. The doctor helped her towards the bed and let her body slump unconsciously on it. She fell into a short sleep.

When she woke up, she found herself tied to the bed. Her legs were fixed to the two lower side belts and her arms were fixed to the other pair of belts. She could move her arms slightly. She was almost naked. Her blouse and skirt lay on the table, her knickers on top of them. Her brassiere was untouched; her breasts were the only covered portion of her body. Suddenly she realized the presence of the two men in the room. A wave of humiliation and fear overcame her and she closed her eyes, grinding her teeth.

'Look here, Nancy,' the doctor said, 'I want to help you. I have no intention of harming you or humiliating you or causing you any irritation. I am a doctor and I do perform my duties as a doctor. Don't feel shy, and please don't fear anything. It will take only two hours, don't fear a thing.'

The doctor's fatherly but unnatural voice softened her. She opened her eyes then closed them.

'Can I do it now? It is better to start early,' he said, filling the syringe. His eyes were on both her and the syringe. She nodded. The doctor gave a triumphant smile, also nodding his head. Magege sighed and moved his chair a little closer to the bed. Nancy took a glimpse at him and rapidly closed her eyes, biting her lower lip in a brave smile. The doctor started the stop clock and went to her, seizing her right thigh. After driving the needle into the flesh, he started to push the brown fluid in the syringe gently into the thigh. She closed her eyes tight and ground her teeth till all the fluid in the syringe was finished. He drew out the needle and swabbed the injected area with methylated spirit. Nancy gave out a deep sigh.

'It is going to be a bit painful, but keep quiet and let it pass gently. We'll be at your side. Many girls can resist it, I have treated more than a hundred up to now and they held it low till the end; you are not different, I hope.' His voice was pleasing and gentle his face was smiling broadly. They were all quiet as the clock covered the room with an irritating tick-tock.

V

Her stomach started to groan wildly. The arm of the clock pointed at eighteen minutes. She grunted with fear. The doctor grinned. She started to feel pain, and the grumbling in her stomach became louder. The pain moved from one end of her belly to the other. As the long arm of the clock moved the grumbling was displaced by successive pains, which moved from one end to the other. Sweat collected on her brow. The pains increased with the tick of the clock. She frowned and, grinding her teeth, twisted her waist following the movement of the intolerable pains. Her breast heaved up and down in a spasmodic motion. She flexed her shoulders and moved both her thighs, closing and opening them. She tried to hold her stomach with her hands but her arms could move only to the height of the edges of the bed; they were tied.

Now the very clock seemed to slow down. The pain exploded mercilessly in her belly. She moaned, tears collected on her smooth cheeks and rolled down softly. She gripped the sides of the bed tightly and jerked her body up and down constantly. The doctor moved and pinned her to the bed. She cursed him and spat in his face vehemently. Magege was still smiling but his smile was stiff and scared. The doctor, sonya'ing angrily, wiped his face and kept her pinned to the bed. Magege, wearing his scared smile, observed blankly as a young girl went through her torment.

Forty five minutes passed. The girl started yelling and calling for her mother, Joseph, Deo and Rosa, asking for help. Constantly she moaned 'Maa-ma, maa...'and she wailed when the pain came to a peak. One hour passed and she began to bleed profusely. Her wails and screams increased. She started to call Joseph's name steadily. The doctor and Magege looked at each other astonished.

'Mr. Magege, call that Joseph here,' Allan ordered, and Magege walked out of the chamber with a trail of screams following him into the consultation room. He met Joseph at the telephone.

'...yes. Independence Avenue, near the IPQ building, a house siding the building to the left. You will see a small sign. Come quickly, please. Yes. Haya.' Joseph put down the phone.

'What are you doing?' Magege asked.

'Oh, I was telephoning a friend,' Joseph answered.

'Ah. It's alright. Come this way, your boss wants you.'

Joseph followed Magege into the room. Shocked, he covered his mouth with his palm in total disbelief as he saw the girl on the bed, the blood in the bowl, and the blood coming from Nancy's body.

'Do you know this girl, Joseph?' the doctor asked. He had to shout to make himself heard above Nancy's cries.

'Yes!' Joseph shouted back. He looked at the two men and walked out of the chamber cursing. Nancy called him back, screamed for him to come back as the tears formed fountains in her eyes. He did not go. He went to the consultation room and sat on a chair, weeping bitterly.

Suddenly, the screams fainted away and were replaced by soft moans. The girl closed her eyes. Her face, so filled with anguish, became dead grey. The doctor stirred, a mask of fear replaced the excited look on his face. He quickly examined Nancy: nothing had come out other than blood.

He dashed to the cupboard, selecting needles with another type of injection bottle. He drew out a red liquid from the bottle and injected it into the girl's left thigh. Nancy continued to moan softly. Her breathing slowed down and her breast heaved no more. Gently, softly, thus she breathed, and the room had fallen into a dead silence.

The door of the chamber burst open. A group of armed policemen surrounded the room, their guns pointed at the two men. One of the invaders was a cameraman. He took several quick snaps.

Magege was taken unawares by the abrupt commotion; he stood with his mouth wide open. A small trail of urine flowed from the tips of his shoes and collected under the bottom of the cupboard. Joseph walked into the chamber. Passing between the two policemen near the bed, he bowed towards the girl and called her by name. Allan glared at him murderously. Nancy opened her eyes and seeing Joseph, she gave a faint smile and said softly, 'Joseph! I am sorry, tell mama I –a-m-s-s…' She closed her eyes and gave a long, tremulous sigh. After a few seconds, Joseph put his palm on her breast. There was no heartbeat.

MOURNES

I

Deo turned over the pages of the Bible, reading a paragraph each time he came across an interesting line. Most of the time he looked at verse. At school he used to write a lot of poetry for the school literacy magazines. He was not a very good poet, but his understanding of a few poets, English and African, stirred an urge in him to create some poems. Even to his own mind he was quite unsuccessful as a poet, nevertheless after working hours, on rare occasions, he wrote for his own enjoyment.

Coming to the psalms, he rushed to those written by David, his favourite. At Psalm 12, he paused, read it to the end and then re-read aloud:

> Help, Lord, for the godly man ceaseth:
> For the faithful fail from among the children of men.
> They speak vanity everyone with his neighbour:
> With flattering lips and with a double heart do they speak.
> The Lord shall cut off all flattering lips, and the tongue that
> speaketh proud things.
> Who have said,
> With our tongue will we prevail;
> Our lips are our own;
> Who is Lord over us?
> For the oppression of the poor,
> For the signing of the needy,
> Now will I arise,
> Saith the Lord:
> I will set him in safety from him that puffeth at him.
> The words of the Lord are pure words, as silver tried in a furnace
> of earth purified seven times.
> Thou shalt keep them, O Lord,
> Thou shalt preserve them from this generation forever.
> The wicked walk on every side,
> When the vilest men are exalted.

Suddenly a wind of excitement aroused him; he perceived the reality of the psalm. The confusion in which he had existed for a long time dwindled fast, like a man's shadow when it approaches noon. So that was it!

'... the wicked walk on every side, when the vilest men are exalted.' He stared at the ceiling, the psalm whistling in his head like a bird unable to take flight. He stared at the ceiling until it painted itself with the words of the psalm. The white ceiling was a large screen; it showed Magege with his fellow sugar daddies sharing a huge table, drinking and talking with contented egos. It was a magnificent assembly. On a stage at the front a number of young girls danced and sang happily, attempting by every fashion to catch the attention of one of Magege's group, 'the vilest men.' On the sides of the stage, a group of older women encircled the young girls clapping their hands to them, but also making gestures attempting to attract the 'exalted men'. In the unoccupied interstices of the big assembly, a young woman would walk, passing aimlessly from one side of the hall and then returning the same way. This one kept her eyes pinned steadily on the table of men.

* * *

'Yes, Frank, the wicked shall walk on every side, and the Lord shall preserve them, when the vilest men are exalted, when the most horrid men are anointed leaders, for the oppression of the poor, for the sighing of the needy, the dirtiest rogues are made bosses!'

He was speaking to Frank, who had opened the door and stood at the corridor which led to the sitting room. Frank was perplexed.

'God forbid. You have not run mad!' Frank said and went straight into the sitting room. He took a seat, slumping his body carelessly into it. Deo opened the page of the Bible which had the Psalm of David. He handed it to Frank and the latter took it, his face showing no interest whatsoever. Frank read from the first line to the last and started the verse over again. Deo moved with him, his eyes also on the psalm, though he had memorized almost all the lines. Frank smiled at Deo as he read the last lines aloud, emphasizing them, understanding dawning in his eyes.

For some minutes they remained silent. Then Frank asked for a cold drink. Deo gave him a bottle of lime juice and Frank served himself. He kept his face averted at all times; he seemed to be trying to avoid Deo's cold stare.

Abruptly Frank spoke. 'But you said you were over with this biblical nonsense,' he started.

'You did not understand me,' said Deo. 'What I meant was that I am no longer tied to the Christian "suffer silently" business. One can be over with Christianity, but still follow some of the arguments in the Bible. If you take this psalm, for example, and forget all about the theology, then review the wording from a certain social point of view, you'll find that a lot has been said. If the psalm says "The Lord shall cut off all flattering lips…", I say, 'the people shall cut off all hypocrites and saboteurs." See this line? It is not the Lord God that I value in this line. I take it that the people, the oppressed will arise and free themselves.'

'And how will you change the last two lines?' Frank asked.

'Ah, for those I will not change at all. It is enough that 'O Lord' is replaced by 'my people.'

Neither of them spoke as Frank drained the juice from his glass. Then Frank looked at Deo and commented, 'I was wondering what the women's organization is doing as far as sexual morals and youth are concerned.'

Deo sighed resignedly. 'Ah. Not many youth know about a women's organization,' he said.

'You are right', Frank admitted, 'and I'm not sure anybody cares whether young people really know about it.' Silence followed, except the soft music from the record player.

'Youth,' Deo took up the thread, 'should be the aim in every movement. The old are old in everything, even in their beliefs and commitments. It is difficult for them to bear a change. To carve a revolution out of the old is like making a Makonde carving out of worm-bored wood. It will not last.'

'You know,' said Frank, 'right now youth are the victims of our society's sex morals, coming and going. Some of the older men are the ones who violate sex morals, and then they lay the blame on youth. Young people trust and accept help and advice from their elders; but the elders have no help to offer. Some give wrong advice, some are opportunistic. The responsible, trustworthy elders do not really understand contemporary youth; when they try to mould the young people along their own lines, they spoil everything...'

'I think,' Deo said, 'only the Youth League, only us, the victims ourselves, can solve our own problems.'

He continued, 'One can sometimes say that youths have many contradictions among themselves, many ills and that many of them are rotten. Yes, this is right, and it is because the big men, the sugar daddies want it that way. Take first the contradictions among us: I am Deo and I am shouting 'Change!' But they give me a good job, a good position, I become one of them, I shout no more. You are Frank and you shout 'Change!' and they give you a good position, and then they take away your position and silence you.

'Mzee Mashaka is shouting 'Change!' But they know he is screaming from deep in the sea, nobody will hear him. He is un-educated, he is "just" a worker; they let him shout on. Now take the rottenness among us. Yes, we are rotten. Look into the streets, into the pombe shops and hotels, look everywhere. We are rotten.

'You are Frank. You have realized that you are rotten, but you are alone. Many have not realized that they are rotten. You go into the street and shout 'We Are Rotten!' The others laugh at you, but let's take it that you are lucky and you get a convert or two, now you become two and your call gets louder, 'We Are Rotten.' Thus you explode. This time the bureaucrats get stirred; somebody is threatening to cut the lucrative flow of film-goers, pombe shop customers, disco goers and jockers, fashion promoters and swingers; somebody is scaring would-be prostitutes and the cities will soon no more be embroidered with female 'flowers' for consumption. Somebody is calling girls to the urban areas and to factories, to produce for the nation, to stand proud as women. Then who will nurse the big hotels and colour entertainment halls with smiles, which will make cities a decadent attraction? So the big men making money out of 'national' enterprises get stirred and rush to their political allies with questions:

"What are you doing? You have let those kids into the street and now they are messing up everything." Then there is a quick, clever, systematic move to silence these "undisciplined" kids. They take the shouting under control and condition it.

Shout but not so loud,
Shout, but keep off your hands,
Shout and your tongue shall replace your hands…

'And it does not end there,' Frank was moved to add. 'The politics of many of these irresponsible "responsible" ones can be thought of as being like that of a certain group of mountaineers. The leaders tell the rest the route they should take, then they themselves take a different path to the top!'

'You are right again,' Deo agreed. 'We know youth cannot make a total change on their own; they have to be under the guidance of a party which represents the people. But why expect youth to follow hypocritical, loudmouth but-actionless advice? When we speak of youths being in the forefront of our national struggles, we can't misinterpret the roles of peasants and workers.

'They are the forces of change, they are the core of everything. But youth, who are also workers and peasants, could trigger everything. They should participate fully as forces of change, as new blood and new energy, they should be always out front.'

Silence. Frank went to the record player and put on an album. He went back to the sofa and served himself another glass of juice. He was becoming more restless as the silence dragged along. Deo looked at him with concerned suspicion.

'But, Frank, since you entered my house you have looked as though you had something special to say. Are you in trouble? What is it? I hope it is not the Swahili woman again. You have seen so much of her…'

'No, it is not the woman,' Frank said, trying to avoid his friend's stare.

'What is it, then?' Deo asked.

The record came to an end. Frank made a halfhearted attempt to rise to select another record, but he immediately slumped back onto the sofa. Deo sighed.

'I have some bad news for you, Deo,' Frank began, after taking a big gulp of juice. Deo looked at him, his eyes enquiring. He put down the Bible and sat upright of the sofa. Frank cleared his throat slightly and looked straight into Deo's face.

'Nancy is dead,' he said simply.

'What?' Deo asked, as if he had not heard him well.

'Nancy died at five this evening after a failed abortion.

Again the Psalm of David covered the room, whistling across the chairs, echoing on the walls and sweeping on the table, bed, everything, like whirlwind preparing for a storm. Deo heard a moaning sound coming from nowhere, going nowhere, and the painful cry of death wailed in lamentation, in unison with David's song.

'Who told you?' Deo asked.

'I was there. I had gone to Independence Avenue for some shopping.

'Suddenly two police cars passed the shop in which I was and came to a halt just a hundred yards or so away. The warning siren was on. So many people rushed to the scene; I was among them. Within no time policemen came out of the building, a low building near IPQ house. They had two well-dressed, middle-aged men in handcuffs. One of them was your manager, Magege. They put them into the police cars and carried them away.'

'And Nancy?'

'Wait. Then an ambulance came and carried the girl out under the police guard.'

'How did you know about the abortion, or that the girl was Nancy?'

'The house. I know it is a private hospital, and there was a boy who stays at Livingstone, I think not far from Nancy's home. He comes to our evening judo classes. He told me the girl's name was Nancy and that she stays at Livingstone. Your manager brought her for the abortion. That boy works for the doctor as a messenger.'

Deo said nothing more, nor did he move until Frank left. It had become dark.

II

'Mami Joseph!' Maria called at the door of Ana's house. The other woman answered from the latrine.

'Come on, Mami Nancy,' she said. Maria walked in and sat on a bed to wait for her hostess. Ana came with an empty pail in one hand and a piece of soap in the other. Water formed lines on her legs, lines which traced back to the short cloth with which she covered the lower portion of her body almost to the knees. She sat on a bed opposite the one on which Maria sat, then she untied the piece of cloth and began to dry the water on her legs.

'Ah!' Ana sighed, 'there was this young school boy of mine who comes here almost daily in the evenings.'

'Do you charge him?' Maria asked.

'Sometimes. But most of the time I let him do it free. I like him, apart from business.'

'Heh, you are strange! I would charge even the youngest kid who crossed my doorsill,' Maria said and they both laughed. Ana slid the makeshift cloth which separated the sleeping area from the rest of the room to the far end of its wire. She dressed and joined Maria on the bed.

'How is business going?' she asked Maria.

'It is good, though today I rejected all the men who knocked at my door,' Maria complained.

'Heh! Why did you? Nowadays I don't let money pass me by. Why didn't feel like working. I feel as if something bad is going to happen to me. May be the police are going to arrest us. You know I am very sensitive to bad things which are going to happen to me.

'Aah! Nothing bad. Many policemen are our daily customers, how can they arrest us? Can a rock rabbit defacate in its own cave?'

A man peeped through the door. Ana told him to come in. He came. He was middle-aged. His clean-shaven chin and handsome face contrasted sharply with the way he was dressed. His dirty brown shirt hung loosely, covering half the hole in the rear of hs trousers. He had a ten-shilling note already in his hand.

'Nafasi?' he asked.

'Nafasi for what?'

'I want a piece from either of you,' he said firmly, his voice very masculine and thick.

'We are two, so come sometime later,' Ana said and the man walked out speechless. The women broke into loud laughter.

'Such firm, manly men!' Maria said.

'Ah,' Ana said, 'men are always men, you open your thighs, they get wild and become brainless like maddened rhinos, when you close the thighs later, the men have softened, they are self-conscious and shy.' Laughter. Ana went to the window to peep at the man as he retreated.

'Is Nancy at home?' Ana asked after sitting back on the bed.

'No. She is out again. She did not come home. Why are you asking?'

'I was just asking. You know, one of these thugs can grab her and rape her if you are not around.'

'Ah. That's the least of my worries,' Maria said. 'At home one is always safe, only her outings scare me.'

'Hodi!' called a boyish voice at the door.

'I guess that is Joseph,' Ana said. 'I was afraid he had decided not to see me anymore.'

'Where is he staying?' Maria asked.

'I don't know. But I remember one day he mentioned to me about having a room at Ilala. I think he stays there or he might still be staying with his friends a few lanes away.'

'You can't keep a son in this trade, I know,' Maria said conclusively.

'Hodi!' the voice called again. Ana told him to come in. Joseph walked in sweating.

'Joseph!' Ana exclaimed with motherly joy. The youth took a small stool and sat down carelessly.

'You are sweating profusely! Where are you coming from at this late hour? It is eight now and thugs are out looking for people to rob and murder.' Ana was talking and searching in the cupboard at the same time, looking for something for her son to eat.

He did not answer. Instead he turned his face, torn with sorrow and fear to Maria.

'Nancy is dead,' he told her. Maria neither moved nor stirred. She did not understand. Ana dropped the teapot in her hands.

'Nancy died today on Independence Avenue. She is now at the mortuary at Muhimbili Hospital. She was attempting an abortion and it failed…'

He explained the whole matter to her, and as he finished Maria fell down in a faint.